TWO TO TAME

Fast and Easy
Taming Tessa

Betty Womack

EROTIC ROMANCE

Siren Publishing, Inc.
www.SirenPublishing.com

A SIREN PUBLISHING BOOK
IMPRINT: Erotic Romance

TWO TO TAME
Fast and Easy
Taming Tessa
Copyright © 2011 by Betty Womack

ISBN-10: 1-61034-535-5
ISBN-13: 978-1-61034-535-4

First Printing: April 2011

Cover design by Jinger Heaston
All cover art and logo copyright © 2011 by Siren Publishing, Inc.

ALL RIGHTS RESERVED: This literary work may not be reproduced or transmitted in any form or by any means, including electronic or photographic reproduction, in whole or in part, without express written permission.

All characters and events in this book are fictitious. Any resemblance to actual persons living or dead is strictly coincidental.

Printed in the U.S.A.

PUBLISHER
Siren Publishing, Inc.
www.SirenPublishing.com

SIREN PUBLISHING *Classic*

Fast and Easy

BETTY WOMACK

FAST AND EASY

BETTY WOMACK
Copyright © 2011

Chapter One

The last time they worked together, Carmen Redstone shot him in the ass.

Denato Genonese never let her live it down. Of course it had been an accident, one he'd caused with hotshot one-upmanship.

She couldn't believe the department had reassigned her to ride with the jerk again.

She never liked him, hated his swaggering ways and the way he took the lead all the time.

Visiting him in the hospital taught her how deep his asshole ways went. The wise guy had ordered her to check her weapon outside the door. He'd grinned, but his cop buddies had a good laugh at her expense.

After that, she'd gone out of her way to avoid him. She'd been roughed up in that drug bust too, but he never mentioned the broken arm she got out of it.

He barely glanced her way when he came into the conference room, his limp a gross exaggeration to remind her of her error in judgment.

She wished her hair would stay put. Tendrils crawled out of the tight bun she rolled it into. The room was hot, and the fine sheen of sweat on her face embarrassed her.

The August heat of Kansas City wasn't the reason for the sweat. Seeing him again brought back inferno-hot memories of the one time they screwed like minks in a cage.

The arrogant bastard in battered jeans and a white polo still raised her temperature. Damn the luck. He came toward her.

"Carmen." He flicked a glance over her. "Captain tell you?"

"Tell me what?" She wasn't about to broach the subject of them working as a team. "I'm sure you're busting to lay it on me."

The habit of resting his hand on the butt of the Glock on his trim waist seemed more of a taunt now. "My partner transferred out to Denver. I'm stuck with you."

This was so like him. He'd been blunt before, but this was pure dung coming from his mouth.

She covered the hurt with as little anger as possible. "Maybe they think you need someone to take over when the heat's on." The drone of the old fan in the corner seemed louder than usual. "I'll see you in the parking lot."

"You can ask for another man to ride with." He reached in his back pocket to pull out his wallet. "I'll buy your lunch, and we can figure out where you want to go."

"Very sensitive of you, Don." She stood and shoved him out of her way. "It takes a man to make me do anything."

"You're looking at him, babe." He stuck the wallet back in his pocket.

He was only a couple inches taller than her five foot eight, but his body was prime muscle and able to back up any threat he made.

"Yeah, I'm looking at a loud-mouthed jerk who can't understand the way this job works."

He gazed at her, the accessing stare familiar. "You can't be lecturing me on procedures?" He flicked a finger at her escaping hair. "You have no idea how to take a man down without killing everyone else."

"Our shift has started." His nasty comments stung. "Let's go, or are you still on disability?"

"You plan to put me back on it?"

He wouldn't let it go. She wasn't going to weasel out and let him tongue lash her.

She remembered his way with that tongue. It had driven her wild. The gleam in his dark eyes assured her he was remembering that fuck. Staked out for two days, she'd gotten bored, and he'd gotten horny. She'd given him everything right there among the fast food boxes and soda cans.

He'd almost passed out with excitement.

"Don." She avoided eye contact with him, picking up her sunglasses and notepad. "I'll see if Captain Wesman will assign you another detective."

That grabbed his attention, and he looked ready to explode. "Not on your life." He lowered his voice as if to make sure she listened to him. "Wouldn't that look great on my record? 'Genoese couldn't handle the stress of partnering with a female.'" He smiled sardonically. "Stay out of my business, Redstone. Unless you want to go on stakeout again." He winked at her. "I'll make an exception for that."

"You couldn't handle it, Genonese." She wasn't going to back off until he did. "Next time, I'll shoot you in your brain pan. That would be your ass."

He shot a dark glare in her direction. "Let's go." He walked ahead of her and ignored the door closing in her face.

Her quick stride got her to their assigned squad car first, and she opened the door to driver's side.

She was hauled back against him as she tried to get in the patrol car. He'd hooked a finger in her belt loop. "Get out." He pulled her back from the car and jerked on the loop several times. "I want to live through the night."

He hadn't touched her since the motel room, but his hands still sent lightning bolts zapping through her. "Get your hands off my ass."

The group of officers a few yards away cut their lively conversation to observe what went on between her and Genonese. There were too many witnesses around to smash him in the face. This would be one long fucking night. She'd make sure it was the last night they spent together.

While he drove, she kept an eye out for the suspects who pulled off a home invasion in the area. For a short time, business replaced anger and they rode in silence.

The Eastside was already hopping with illegal activity. Hookers prowled the streets, and dealers waited for drug heads wanting a fix. They melted into the shadows as the dark blue sedan rolled past.

The computer on the console lit up. She tensed with expectation.

"Two of our suspects were seen in the east bottoms, camping out on a sand bar."

"Give me a better location, Redstone."

"You know Cat Bridge." She'd taken in a couple of the throwaway cats and knew the treacherous footing under the bridge. "City Market and Fifth Street."

He glanced her way. "You're not dressed to go mudding." He looked at the dash clock and gestured to her white slacks. "I'll take you to your apartment and you can change into jeans."

He was right, but that would give their home invaders time to be tipped off the law was on to them.

"Forget my clothes. Let's go." She grimaced at the thought of chasing a couple of fleet-footed jack-offs through mud and weeds.

"Don't say I didn't ask." Don made a fast u-turn and grinned at the scowl she threw in his direction. "You're really cute when you're pissed."

"You'll think I'm downright gorgeous if you turn this thing over."

He laughed, speeding toward the downtown district. She sensed his adrenalin rush and had to admit, she liked taking freaks off the street.

She checked her seatbelt and called in their location to the midtown precinct. Hearing these guys' rap sheets from dispatch, she knew taking them down wouldn't be easy. Hell, nothing about this job was easy.

Don glanced at her again, wheeling around slower traffic. "You got running shoes on?"

"Of course." She pulled her feet back against the set. "Keep your eyes on the road."

Why the hell had she dressed like an undercover vice cop? White slacks and kidskin heels?

"Aw, shit." He groaned and hit the steering wheel. "See, that's what I get for hooking up with you. Four inch heels on this job."

"What's wrong? Is that more than you're packing?" She was tempted to hit him in the gut, but that could wait.

He looked straight ahead and drove around the groups of young people that frequented the trendy bars downtown. His mood became cold calculation, and his voice matched that mood when, as always, he took the lead.

"We get out at the bridge and hike down the riverbank." He parked the car at the end of the footbridge that led to the overgrown shoreline. He got out of the car and dropped the keys in his pocket. "Be quiet. If you have anything to say, do it now."

"I will if you will." She got out and stood beside him, checking the clip in her weapon. "I won't be chit-chatting with you anytime soon." She jammed the Glock back into the holster on her belt.

He grabbed her hand, taking the flashlight she'd brought. "I'll man the lights." He walked ahead of her.

"Are you sure you can handle it?"

He looked back at her and stopped. He put his arm around her shoulders. "Don't make me show you here on this muddy riverbank." He groaned softly. "Pipe down and follow me."

* * * *

Carmen Redstone drove him crazy. Don listened to her grumbling comments, his gut telling him this was a big mistake. She was too busy hating him to keep her mind on the job at hand.

No, that wasn't true. He knew she was all cop when the chips were down. He couldn't let his feelings for her get in the way. Carmen wouldn't leave his mind since their night of ball busting sex in that sleazy motel. It seemed like a wall of fire had exploded around them, and no matter what happened, they were going to have hot, crazy sex.

After she put a bullet in his ass during a kiddy porn bust, he convinced himself he was too pissed to ever think of her in a favorable way again.

Hell, he knew that was just a way to ease his growing desire to have her under him again. She'd been doing her job, and he'd tried to shield her from gunfire and got in the way.

He almost reached the point she didn't haunt him, and now they were together again. And she was grinding her way back into his groin.

A sound from down river caught his attention, bottles being broken against the snags and rocks. He stopped, and Carmen bumped up against his back. He instinctively took a deep breath and reached back to steady her. "That may be our men."

"Too close." She listened intently, patting his back. "Probably fishermen or kids smoking pot."

"Could be." He moved ahead and turned the flashlight on, lighting the path. "Why don't you stay here in case they run back this way?"

Her silence didn't fool him. She was seething.

"Why don't you stay here and let me handle this?" He could almost hear her teeth gritting over her comment.

"Okay, we can talk about this at my place." He hooked his arm around her slender waist. "We can have one hell of a fight."

"That's not necessary. You already know what a sweetheart you are." She pushed his arm away. "Let's get this done."

He shrugged off her comments, hearing the same crap from every dealer and molester he arrested. But coming from her, it carried some weight.

She stuck close, her perfume wafting around him to take his mind off the stink of the river and decaying weeds. His lusty thoughts burst after she stumbled and sent a ton of loose rocks rumbling down the riverbank.

"Can you make any more noise, Redstone?" He forced his voice to a low hiss.

She jabbed a finger against his back. "That could just as well be something more lethal in your back." Her sweet personality vaporized, instantly morphing her into a hardnosed cop. From the corner of his eye, he saw her touch the weapon on her belt. "There they are, on that sandbar."

He looked up, grateful for the moonlight. "I'll go first. You stop them if they get past me."

"Oh, sure. I'm going for that." She snorted in that cute way she did if she was really disgusted. "In your wet dreams, partner."

"Don't argue, Redstone." He turned to look at her. "I need you for backup. Shut up and take cover."

"Which is it?" Her whisper was like a dagger in his gut. "Hide or cover your sorry ass?"

"Let me write this down. You're an obstinate little mule."

She stood toe to toe with him, hands on her hips, and her chin lifted in a stubborn angle.

"Oh hell, come on." The light wasn't good, but he saw the grin of victory. He became distracted, remembering how her lips tasted and felt.

He was a fool for considering sleeping with her again, but the memory of her sweet body was getting to him, and he couldn't do a damn thing about it.

Not right now, anyway. But, the night was young.

Chapter Two

Carmen picked her way down the rocky slope, losing the heel of her right shoe. She stopped long enough to break off the other heel and hurried to catch up with Don.

"What were you doing back there?" He snorted with derision. "Not tired are you? Afraid, maybe?"

She jumped when a black cat ran across the weedy path. "The only thing I'm afraid of is your lousy attitude getting me killed."

He apparently didn't mind being called on his personality. It suited him so well. "Ouch."

"Be still." He clamped his hand over her mouth and whispered in her ear. "I see the headlights of a car downstream on that old boat loading ramp."

"So let's check it out."

Roughly he her pushed aside and left her standing in ankle deep water as he headed downstream.

"Damn you, Don. You're not leaving me here." Following him at a dead run had to be a nightmare. Stumbling over rocks and stepping into sucking mud, she caught up with him a few yards from the ramp.

He motioned for her to get down, his way of saying he'd handle the situation. She grudgingly complied, knowing he'd seen someone in the car.

"That's not a man in the car." He chuckled. "It's a couple of babes."

"What?" Carmen stood, and pressed close to him. "What are they doing?"

"Getting head."

"Did you see the John in there?"

Don pressed his finger to her lips. "It's just two Johnettes." He took her hand and led Carmen away from the car. "I could never mess up a man's, err, a chick's come. That would be cruel and unusual."

"Cruel, my ass." She took a step back toward the car. "They're breaking the law. What if some guy walks by here with his kids?"

"Fat chance of that happening." Don slapped at his neck. "Who's going to bring kids out here? These mosquitoes are a lot more dangerous than two chicks getting it on."

She wanted to rip him a new one, but instead lost her footing and slid down into the muddy water. Buffeted by branches and trash coming downriver, she grabbed for anything that would keep her near the bank.

"Don!" She choked on a mouthful of the disgusting bilge and spit it out. "Don!"

She heard splashing close by before she saw him. He was there, running out to where she fought to keep her head up. He grabbed her around the waist and hauled her to shore.

"Help a little here." He stumbled and went down, taking her with him. She would have laughed, but she was a little afraid he'd let go of her. He managed to slog out of the water, pulling her along like a sack of potatoes. "Here we go again."

She didn't care what he said. Nothing had ever felt better than the mud under her back, and she wasn't interested in him at the moment.

A few minutes passed before curiosity made her ask what he'd meant. "Were you making a chauvinist comment about me, Don?"

"Hell, yes." He rubbed water out of his eyes and pointed at her nose. "You're a fucking menace, Redstone."

She sat up and twisted her sopping hair into a long ponytail. "I hear you, and thanks for dragging me out." She was grateful for that, but his continual little digs dimmed her desire to be nice to him.

He stood, checking to see if he still had his weapon and shield. "If you're finished wasting time, let's find those high-class bastards." He swiped at the mud on his jeans. "Lord, what a night."

"I agree."

"With what?"

"That you're a nice guy when you have to be." She scrambled to her feet and headed out onto the sandbar.

She heard his footsteps behind her, glad he'd covered her back. The sandbar was soft, and she sank past her shoe tops. She hated to admit he'd ever been right about anything, but going home for a fast change of clothes would have been the smart thing to do.

Hearing men's voices, she stopped. "They're at the end of the outcrop." Pulling out her Glock, she bent down to wait for Don to talk over their plan of action.

"I don't think we should take them completely by surprise." He squatted next to her. "I say we go with plan one."

"The one where you play sheriff and I show up as Gabby Hayes?" His soft groan made her reword her comment. "Okay, you let them know you're here. I'll bring up the rear." She rolled her eyes, and watched as he moved ahead.

She followed, staying several steps behind him. He walked along the edge of the bar, gripping his weapon in both fists.

Damn, why didn't he say something? The felons had stopped talking and doused their lantern. They obviously knew the cops were there.

"It's the KCPD, boys. Put your hands on your heads and walk toward us." Don yelled his orders, but the men on the sandbar remained silent.

All hell broke out after that. Glass breaking, gunfire and screaming rolled up the river and twisted her nerves into stretched barbed wire.

With no light to see where they were, Carmen stood her ground in the middle of the narrow island, bending her knees for better leverage.

She heard Don ordering them to drop their weapons and hit the dirt. From that point on, everything was a mix of cursing and more gunfire. Someone ran toward her.

He was fat, gaining ground, and carrying a gun. Asshole number one was hell bent on getting by her, aiming for a full tackle if she didn't move. She froze where she was, yelling at him to halt. He opened his mouth and let out a scream, leveling his pistol at her.

Come on scumbag.

He was two feet away when she made her move, stepping to her right and taking him down with a foot to his knee.

He screamed in pain, rolling onto his belly. "You bitch! You broke my knee." The weapon he'd brandished at her flew off to the side and thudded into the sand.

She knelt down and yanked his hands behind his back, gritting her teeth as she forced the cuffs on his wrists. "Calm down, Princess, or I'll give you something to cry about."

Don walked back to where she held her arrest down with a knee to his backbone. "You all right, Redstone?"

She looked behind him. "Where's yours?"

"He's lying back there with a broken nose." He pulled out a well-worn card and read the detainee his rights. She knew the guy didn't hear any of it over his cussing and threats. After shoving the card in his pocket, he called in their location.

They didn't talk much while waiting for transport. It had gone down pretty sloppy in her eyes, but both of them were alive and these two creeps would spend a lot of time in jail.

Carmen watched Don check on his bloodied prisoner. She heard him comment on the danger of using drugs, his version of light humor. The guy didn't laugh. The packets of drugs taken from his pants pockets would add some time to his sentence.

She wasn't too concerned about the guy. He felt well enough to hold the rag Don had found and shoved at him to his bleeding nose.

While Don checked the downed man over, she focused on his hands. They were strong and tanned, and she remembered how they'd touched and stroked every part of her. He knew her body as well as she did. He leaned over the screaming man, and she flushed hot, remembering him leaning over her, making her wait while his cock pulsed between her quivering thighs.

"Redstone."

"Yeah."

"Transport's coming."

The wail of sirens burst her erotic dream. "Maybe we can get out of here without much trouble." She stood, watching the flickering lights at the footbridge.

Don handed her the flashlight. "You want to go meet them?" He gestured to her prisoner. "They're not going anywhere."

She didn't balk or argue. After all, they were partners, if only for tonight. "The arrest report will take hours."

"After we're finished with them, we'll go clean up." He looked at his watch, the glow of the dial clear in the humid darkness. "If we're lucky, we'll be done by the end of our shift."

Okay. He's not reporting you for any missteps. Does he want to work with you after all?

"I'll go get the report started."

"Carmen."

She paused in mid-step. "Yeah."

"Good job." He dropped the car keys in her hand.

She flushed at his unexpected praise. "Thanks, Don. It was a good bust."

Her warm glow faded with every step toward the bridge.

You're an idiot, Carmen. A few decent words from him and you're ready to roll over. He'd say that to one of these wild cats just for conversation.

She walked a short distance back with the officers and EMC's until she was sure they would find Don and the drug dealers.

While she climbed the narrow steps to the street, several residents of the tent city near the bridge approached her. She caught a whiff of their stench, figuring it wouldn't take a breathalyzer test to know they had been on the bottle recently. Kittens that had been peeping out from under the footbridge took off for safety.

"We got wine." The taller of the two held out a bottle that was running on empty. "Take a drink." He cackled, and punched his companion in the ribs. "You can be our woman tonight."

Okay. This is getting serious.

"Sorry boys, but I'm still on duty." Carmen took her shield from her belt and held it up. The piece of metal seemed to sober them up in a hurry.

They mumbled an incoherent apology and stumbled their way under the bridge. She breathed a sigh of relief, glad they were able to figure out what the shield meant.

She knew Don was close when she heard gravel crunching under his shoes.

"Who were you talking to?" He waited for her to get in the car. "You drive."

"You're kidding?" Her brows lifted in exaggerated shock.

"I'm not." He got into the passenger seat and belted himself in. "I think I pulled a groin muscle fighting that prick."

She got in the car, buckling up before speaking to him. "We can stop at the emergency room if you need it."

He shook his head, and drying mud from his hair flew over the dashboard. "I'm too tired for that. Take me to a nice hot shower and dry shorts."

Carmen laughed, eyeing his hair that stood in muddy spikes off his scalp. "Your place or mine?"

She couldn't snatch back the evocative suggestion. Hell, she didn't want to.

"Your place is closer." He grinned and leaned his head back against the headrest. "I may want to nap while I'm there."

"I don't recall inviting you for a sleepover."

"We didn't sleep, remember?"

Her nerves tightened down to her crotch. Remember? She hadn't had a decent relationship since they'd torn the motel bed down.

She signed the report and handed him the clipboard, nearly climaxing when he grinned and grabbed her hand to kiss her fingers.

"Just write your report, you charmer." He heaved an exaggerated sigh and turned on the overhead light. "We can expect to be called in by IA after the hospital turns in their report."

"Fuck IA." He wrote fast and steady, obviously not concerned with what would happen. Frankly, neither was she. They had handled the arrest in a professional manner.

She watched him sign the four-page document and slide the pen in the top of the clipboard. "Let's get this over with, Don. I'm turning into a brick."

He laughed and patted her thigh. "We'll have to scrape this stuff off."

"Were you serious about going to my place?" Oh damn. She had to open her mouth and sound like a desperate slut. "I meant that you don't have any clothes at my apartment."

"How about you stopping at my apartment, and I'll grab some clean stuff." He turned the air condition on high. "Okay with you, Redstone?"

"Sure."

Good going, Carmen. You have positively proven how horny you are. Well, he doesn't need to know it's him you've been burning for.

Chapter Three

At headquarters, Carmen stood rigid with resentment as the captain barked out his questions while reading from their reports. "What do you mean, their rights?" She didn't miss the warning that flashed in his blue eyes, yet she had to make her statement. "Nothing was violated down there on that sandbar. They had drugs and alcohol and fired weapons at us."

Don grinned at her and touched his throat in a slicing motion. "We read them the Miranda, gave first aid, and called for the EMT's." He roughed his hair and little pellets of mud shot across the room.

She hoped the interrogation hadn't dampened his desire for hot sex. She needed to blow off steam, and he was the only one who could help her hit the release button.

Captain Wesman paced the floor several times, checking their report again. "Did you find it necessary to cripple the man, Redstone?"

She almost laughed but held it in. "I found it the most effective action if I wanted to stay live. He'll walk again."

Captain Wesman looked like a man that would be more comfortable at home, watching a ball game with his family, not railing at them. He had a thatch of wavy, steel gray hair and a hint of a paunch over his belt. What he'd lost in physical fitness, he'd maintained in his voice of authority.

He nodded, flipping the folder shut. "Internal Affair's will want more from both of you." Wesman glanced at her muddy ensemble "Your shift is over."

"Yes, sir." Carmen avoided eye contact with the stern man on her way out of the room.

Her thoughts weren't on the report. She wanted to run out of the building and hurry to her apartment. A quiver of excitement jangled through her. The rest of the night would be hers, far removed from bums and dealers.

She still couldn't believe they had stopped off at Don's apartment, and he'd come running with fresh clothing under his arm. He was anxious as her to give in to the torrid sex that had been put on hold for months.

He followed her down the quiet hall to the entrance, out the parking lot and to her car. He shook his head and patted her ass. "You still got balls."

She unlocked her door and turned to face him. "I have something better." The light touch of his fingers on her breast switched on a red-hot lick of desire in her pussy. "It's going to set yours on fire."

His soft laugh fueled the flames in her blood. He strode off to his car.

She drove sanely to her apartment, resisting the urge to run lights and break speed limits. He was on her bumper, the idea making her squirm. She wanted to ride his bumper and hear him beg for more.

He pulled behind her in front of her building, getting out of his car before she could open her door.

"Give me the key." He cradled the bundle of clothes under his arm and held his hand out.

"Anxious, are we?" Carmen got out and handed him her keys.

He took her hand and led her to the entrance, turning the key in his fingers with calm deliberation. "I don't want you to leave me standing out here."

She didn't care what he'd meant. The only thing she had planned was wrapping herself around his warm, hard body.

He'd never been in her apartment, and he waited until she pointed him in the right direction. He held her hand while he unlocked the door, pulling her inside with him.

She heard the door slam behind them, and felt the strength of his arms hauling her snug against him. From that point, desire rendered her a little crazy.

His mouth crushed down over hers, his tongue demanding entry. She didn't need coaxing, her lips parted, softening under his until their tongues met in passionate exploration. He was dominating, powerful and rough, pressing her to the wall.

Her panties were wet, and the scent of arousal permeated the warm air. In her passionate stupor, the sound of ripping material jolted her to dreamy sanity. What did she care about popping buttons and ripping material? The zipper of her slacks cried out in protest under his rough treatment, but gave in with a high-pitched whine as her slacks fell to the floor.

His moan spurred her into action, her fingers freeing the belt around his lean waist, working deftly to unbutton his jeans. Pushing her hand down and over his hard belly into his shorts aroused wildness in her. He was hard as blue steel and growing in her hand, beads of pre-come wetting her palm.

She pushed her hips against his hand, spreading her legs to give him all the room he needed to massage her clit. She lifted her leg to his waist, holding him closer to better enjoy the stretching of her pussy around his fingers.

Cool air licked over her bare breasts until his warm palm covered her nipple, his fingers squeezing the taut bud into a sensitive point.

He caught her hand and rasped against her mouth. "You're going to make me explode in your hand." He kissed her hard and sucked her lower lip into his mouth, nipping lightly. "Damn, Redstone. You're fucking hot even with mud on your face."

She squeezed his cock again, and laughed. "Come on dirty boy." She pulled away from him and headed for the bathroom. "I'll let you wash me."

They stripped on the way to the shower, dropping what clothes they still wore onto the floor. Don caught her in his arms, hungrily kissing her, dipping his head to suck her nipples. She didn't have to see his cock to know it stood up tight against his belly. The hot bulge plastered against her skin spurred her into a frenzy of passion with the need to have him inside her.

Somehow they moved to the shower stall, and he turned on the water. It was cool, but didn't extinguish the blazing heat engulfing her.

Carmen locked her arms around his neck, holding him close. He had his wits about him evidently, finding her shampoo in the caddy above her head. She closed her eyes and savored his hands washing her scalp and body. They slid over her ass to her crotch, his fingers stroking her folds and clit, finally sliding inside her pussy.

"Find anything in there?" Her voice was husky with desire, legs tensed with need to release her building climax.

"Just checking." He nuzzled her neck, dropping a bar of soap into her palm.

"Checking for what?" She always wished she didn't have to question his every motive, but it was just part of their relationship. "Find it?"

"Yeah, still tight as a drum and ready to be kissed."

She rolled the soap over several times in her hands, working up a thick lather. Taking her time, she spread the bubbles over his chest and stomach, slowly lathering up his neck and shoulders. Her pussy clenched with raw desire as she watched the trail of bubbles settle around the base of his cock.

"Are you satisfied with what you see, Redstone?"

It took all her willpower, but she turned her back and rinsed her hair, trying to forget how hot she was for him. "I'll let you know after we take it for a test run." She looked over her shoulder, a tiny smirk on her lips. "It's been a while. Something might have changed."

She shivered in the tide of desire whipping through her body. He pressed against her, cupping his hands over her breasts, nipping her earlobe.

The heat of his cock against her ass burned a trail of sizzling need to her throbbing pussy, clenching onto his fingers he dipped inside her.

"Redstone, I think you want me." His deep voice crooned into her ear, and his muscled thighs molded to hers as his fully-loaded dick flicked her ass.

He turned her to face him, teasing her lips with his tongue. Her body was slick inside and out, quivering with raging desire to be under him.

She gripped him, working her fingers along the rigid, veined length until his mouth crushed down over hers in an assault of passion. "I know you want me, Don."

"I'm ready to come, so stop with the hand job, gorgeous." He turned off the water, reaching for the towels hanging on the bar outside the shower stall door and quickly wrapped one around her.

Carmen dried her hair as well as she could while he backed her against the wall to plunder her mouth with his tongue. She shivered, not with cold, but anticipation. Her voice was a shaky whisper. "I want you to come, but not here."

He lifted her in his strong arms and carried her to the bed. She was dazed with passion and erotic yearning. He smelled of her soap and his own spicy scent, warm and seductive.

They fell onto the bed where she collapsed in a heap of helpless delight, laughing while he spread her legs to bury his face in her pussy.

The tease of his tongue searching for her clit set her ablaze. Her laughter became a loud moan of exquisite passion. His hands slipped under her to squeeze her ass and pull her up to his mouth.

The torture of building excitement enslaved her whole being. Surrender was her only emotion as he sucked her clit and drove his tongue deep into her. She clawed his shoulders and locked her legs around his back.

She came, and came, twisting away but holding him fast to the flame. Consumed in fire, she screamed out in the wild fury of release, falling back against the pillows in the aftermath of the storm.

* * * *

Don had to have her, bury his cock as far in her as possible. He'd never forgotten her passion, and tonight she was a hundred times hotter. His shoulders and back burned from her scratching, but the pleasure numbed the pain.

"Damn, Carmen, you're a wildcat." He needed no help finding her pussy, his dick centering instantly on her throbbing entrance. She held her arms up, pulling him down to lie on her. He knew it sounded Neanderthal, but all he could manage was a growl against her ear.

He couldn't slow down and knew she was ready to come again. She was ready, his drive into her hot and tight. She clenched around him, grinding her hips until she cried out again. Pushing forward, he rocked against her until she lifted her hips to pull him deeper, moving in rhythm with his fast, hard stokes. He couldn't breathe, yet the pounding blood coursing through his body kept him going. It blew him away, his orgasm powerful and brilliant behind his eyes.

She clung to him, kissing his neck and shoulders in spent passion, sighing with contentment. He rolled to his side and pulled her close.

"You're beautiful, Redstone."

Her eyes opened slowly, her smile mocking. "You don't have to play me with drink and pretty words, Don."

He exhaled roughly, wanting to shake her. "Why do you do that?"

She lifted up on her elbow. "Do what?"

There was a hint of anger in her voice. "Can't a guy ever get nice with you?"

"Not you, Genonese."

He had no answer for that comment. After all the time he'd blamed her for putting him in the hospital, all the macho quips he'd sent her way, she still had more balls than he did.

"There's got to be a story behind that." He brushed her hair from her forehead.

"You don't need to know my life history." She moved with cat-like grace, straddling his waist to stare darkly at him. "Are you bored already?"

"Hell no, baby." What was she thinking, planning in that evil brain? "Forget I asked."

"No." She leaned back and then laughed. "I watched my pop beat my mom all my life, ran when he'd whip his belt over his head, buckle end out when he was drunk. Which was most of the time."

Don had never heard Carmen reveal anything personal before. He wanted to hug her, but she sat rigid as stone on him. He didn't interrupt her as she spilled the rest of her past.

"Pop taught me one thing that was useful. Not to be afraid of guns and how to fire them." Her shoulders relaxed the longer she talked. "When he died in a gutter, we didn't cry. We were relieved." She grinned at him. "Sounds awful to you, doesn't it?"

"Not that he died, just the part about how he treated you and your mother."

"A girl wants a father to love, Don." She slid off his hips and lay down beside him. "I didn't want to be tough and fire guns."

Propping up on the pillows, he thought about her hard ass attitude. Now he knew where it came from. "It wasn't a waste, Redstone. You're one hell of a cop."

"Yeah, and it sure goes good with eating Christmas dinner alone and singing happy birthday to yourself." She threw a pillow against his face. "Fuck it."

She got up and went to the doorway. He wanted her to stay in bed with him. "Don't run off mad, beautiful."

"You have never seen me mad." Grabbing her robe off a chair, she spoke matter-of-factly. "Want coffee or to get drunk as hell?"

"Your call, babe." He couldn't help being crazy about her. She was too fascinating to ever forget.

Chapter Four

Carmen groaned, a major headache pounding in her temples.

Why had she tried to match him shot for shot?

The aroma of fresh brewed coffee tantalized her nose. Don had entertained her until dawn and showed her he hadn't lost a thing.

"Hey, Redstone." He popped his head around the door to grin at her. "I always have coffee before sex."

Now he was the old Genonese, cocky as hell and a pain in her ass. "In that case, you'd better drink a pot full." She wished her tongue hadn't loosened up with him, but it was too late to worry about.

He wasn't put off, his lean body propped against the door as he teased her. "I can wait, but I don't know about you."

"Kiss my ass, Don." She sat up and stretched her arms over her head. He was still leering at her, making her body flush with pleasure. "What's with you? Never seen a naked woman before?"

"Not like this one." He took a step toward the bed.

"Hold it, Detective." She slid off the bed and pointed to the empty scotch bottle on the floor. "You didn't have to get me plastered to have sex."

"Yeah, maybe." He picked up the shirt he'd brought and put it on, slowly buttoning it. "I have to run, babe. You going to get up to see me off?"

Run? Run where? To whom?

The bubble she'd played around in popped with a painful jab of reality. She'd asked for it, latching onto him with no thought of him leaving.

She shrugged and tried to not sound petulant. "You're probably already late."

He paused a half second before clipping his shield and weapon on his belt. "I'll see you later."

"Sure." Carmen snuggled down in the sheets and turned her back to him. "Be sure to lock the door."

He nodded and left the room. She heard the refrigerator door close and the clink of a spoon in his coffee cup. He was still here, and she wanted to see him, even if it was for just a minute.

She got up and pulled on her robe, hurrying to the kitchen. Her heart almost flipped, seeing him leaning against the sink, smiling at her in that damn sexy way.

"Coffee lure you out here?" He held his cup out to her. "You want to talk?"

She waved the cup away, licking her lips. She felt tongue-tied bringing up the subject. "Are you going to Major Green's retirement party?"

He glanced away then back at her. "No, I'm tied up that night. How about you?"

"No." She picked a lie from the air. "I'm scheduled to work that day."

He set the cup on the counter and took a couple steps toward the door. "What's the real reason you aren't going? Major Green thinks the sun sets in your ass."

"Maybe it does, and you'd better remember that." She threw a dishtowel in his direction. "Get out."

Before she could take a breath, he was back, wrapping his arms around her, his mouth clamping down on hers in a hard kiss. She trembled with desire. She hadn't gotten enough of Don and never would.

He swatted her ass and stepped back, a smart alec grin on his face. "I only remember that ass pumping me dry."

He walked out, and the emptiness of the apartment closed in around her. "I'd love to put a hex on you, Genonese."

She poured coffee in the cup Don had used, turning it to the spot his lips had been on. Now that he was gone, she gave thought to the retirement party she was supposed to attend. Downtown, posh hotel and her showing up with no date. Wouldn't she be just the one?

Pissed off at her situation, she tossed the coffee in the sink.

Why did you bring it up? He cut you off at the ankles. Damn it!

Out of habit, she put the cup in the dishwasher and shut the door. There was nothing in the racks but a saucer and two spoons.

What a life, Carmen. You'll be talking to yourself if you don't make some changes and soon.

Glancing in the bathroom, she grimaced at the mess they had left. Wet towels and ripped clothing lay in heaps on the floor. She gathered the discarded clothing, and dropped them in the washer.

Remembering Don hadn't taken anything with him, she searched for his jeans. They were in the living room, and his shirt had found a home on the sofa.

Just holding his clothing, stained with mud and filthy water gave her a thrill.

She removed the towels from the washer and tossed in his things. While they washed, she sat on the counter and thought about the sound of his voice, the bronze tone of his fine body, head to toe.

While she'd been working him into another round of sex, she'd found the ugly scar from the slug she'd put in him, and nearly gasped at the sight. There would always be that reminder of the pain she'd caused him.

Disgusted with the path her thoughts had taken, Carmen hopped down and went into the living room. She picked up her phone and then dropped it onto the coffee table.

You were ready to call him, weren't you? Fool.

Fast and Easy 31

Going to her closet, she tried to push Don out of her thoughts. The hangers squeaked and grated on the pole as she searched for a decent dress. She had to have something appropriate for the major's party.

Hell no. Everything she owned was either backless, strapless, or thigh-high creations. In the mess were some even shorter skirts. The floor, littered with shoes, told the same tale, all inappropriate just like their owner.

Maybe she'd wear her uniform. That would be a kick in the ass. Whatever the hell she wore, she wasn't staying long. She would be all set gift wise with a box of Monte Christos. The major was such a sweet guy, helping her out of plenty of hot situations.

Shutting the closet door, she thought about Don's comment. What had he meant by that crack about the sun setting in her ass? She'd never gotten the slightest inkling Major Green played favorites with her. Don was a typical male, reading crap into everything.

Too bad he couldn't read her emotions. They would both be a lot happier if he could. Then again, maybe not.

She showered and dressed, putting the wet clothes in the dryer before heading off to find a decent dress. She rolled her eyes at the idea.

For the next several days, Carmen was forced to have a recruit ride with her. Genonese was doing his annual weapons proficiency test and had been testifying in a murder trial. She missed him like fury, but being away from Don for a few days gave her a chance to think of something else.

Time seemed to drag, yet the evening of the reception came all too soon for her. She dressed in her new cocktail dress and piled her hair into a reasonably stylish do. She gave up trying to appear perky and let the stubborn strands around her cheeks do as they pleased.

Where had the time gone?

Why hadn't she had her hair done in a salon? Shoes, she had tons of, but she settled for her standbys, white sandals with three-inch heels.

It was time to leave the comfort of her apartment and head to the Plaza where all the in people hung out.

That was a laugh. She'd arrested most of them for drunken driving or wife beating.

Lord, don't let this night drag on too long.

* * * *

Remembering several unexplained scrapes on the fender of her car, Carmen wasn't anxious to use valet parking. She reluctantly handed over the keys to her Lincoln to an attendant and went inside the discreetly lit lobby of the hotel. Following the signs, she found the banquet room and stood near the exit.

She hadn't been sure about the white silk cocktail dress, but after seeing what the other women were wearing, she relaxed. The dress had cost her a week's pay, but the soft swirl of the skirt around her knees had convinced her to buy it. She was confident the feminine, draped bodice was modest, and the tiny straps would hold her breasts in place.

Lifting her bare shoulders, she moved through the crowd, smiling at the officers she knew, and exchanged a few words with some of them. They all had dates, or their wives hung onto their arms in a territorial stance.

Carmen moved on, finally spotting the guest of honor. She held her hand out. "Congratulations, Major."

He pulled her into the circle of his arms for a hug. "Thank you, Redstone." He smiled and turned to the group of men with him. "You all know Detective Redstone, don't you?" He eyed her dress with a smile. "She's an exemplary officer and is going places in the department."

Knowing some of the men thought she wasn't qualified for advancement, heat rose to her cheeks. After the incident with Genonese, she was considered poison, a joke. "You're too kind,

Major." To change the subject, she pressed the cigars into his hand. "I hope you still like these."

He grinned and held the box up for the others to see. "She knows a good thing when she sees it. Thank you, Carmen."

The others agreed, gathering around, and quickly drew the retiring man back into their conversation. It was a good time for her to think about leaving the scene.

A waiter hoisting a tray loaded with champagne came toward her. She stopped him. "I'll have one of those."

He nodded, holding the tray down for her. The guy was in a hurry, but she didn't miss his male perusal of her legs.

The night wasn't a total loss. Score one. Tipping the flute up to take a sip, her good mood froze solid.

Genonese stood in a corner with his arm around the waist of a redhead in a green dress.

No, oh no. You're not going to let this slide by.

She pasted on a smile and worked her way to where he leaned against a wall. He didn't notice her for several seconds, wrapped up in a bragging session, no doubt.

The redhead saw her first and moved closer to Don's side, a smug little smile on her puss.

Carmen itched to push the chick aside but kept a tight rein on her temper until he caught sight of her.

"Carmen." He dropped his hand from his date's waist and turned red under his tan. "I thought you weren't coming."

She faced him, taking his arm in a firm grip. "That's right, partner. I came over here to see if it was the same guy that lied in my face after we'd fucked all night." The idiot touched her shoulder in a flirtatious way, a grin curving his lips. She brushed at his hand and lowered her voice. "Don't do that again, Genonese."

He mumbled some kind of lame apology to the girl he was with, and stepped away from the group. "Redstone, I forgot I'd set this up weeks ago."

"For a cop, you have a short memory." Carmen smiled at him and whispered, her comments for his ears alone. "You're a liar and a special kind of pig."

"Redstone, you're flying off in all directions." He reached for her arm. Her glare obviously changed his mind, and he withdrew his hand.

"Go back to your lady friend. She looks like she's just been mugged." Carmen glanced around before verbally slashing him again. "I'll see your sorry ass at work. Oh yeah, you'll find your damn jeans on the trash heap."

It was hot in the crowded room, and all she could think about was that snake in the grass. She felt like a fool, never considering Don would already have a date. The idea infuriated her all over again. He didn't have enough balls to tell her.

He was like every other man she'd known. She couldn't trust him.

Hell with it. The music sucked, the champagne warm, and the man who jerked her around was following her.

"Redstone, wait a minute."

"I don't have a minute, Don." She let those little moonbeam feelings creep in while he gazed intently at her. "I have somewhere to be and I'm late."

"That's bullshit." He curved his arm around her waist. "You'll just have to sleep with me after you hear my side of this." He grinned. "Kind of makeup sex."

"Go have it with the dumb chick whose eyes are glaring a hole in your back." Carmen hated the turmoil of jealous hurt that knotted her stomach. "I don't like being lied to."

Damn him! He didn't even try to make up some lame excuse, or follow her as she moved away, weaving her way back to where Major Green stood.

If she hadn't been so caught up in her miserable self pity, she'd have paid more attention to the man who pushed her aside, running straight toward the major.

The flash of exploding powder jolted her into action. Her hand went into the silly evening bag she carried to yank out her snub-nosed thirty-eight. She ran to kneel by her friend who lay wounded. "Is there a doctor here?" She checked the Major's pulse, relieved to feel the strong beat under her fingers. She tried to make herself heard over the noise. "This man needs help right now."

A grim-faced officer worked feverishly, pressing a handful of fancy dinner napkins to the bleeding wound.

She barely heard the shouts and commotion of the other officers taking the shooter down and dragging him from the reception area.

Major Greene groaned and tried to sit up. "Hell, I'm only winged, Carmen. Don't look so worried." He laughed and clutched his arm. "Looks like he ruined my best jacket."

Hearing him joke about it, she breathed normally and patted his shoulder. "You can always get a new coat." He was in pain, no matter how he tried to hide it. "Relax, Major. The EMT's are here."

"There's plenty of party time left, Carmen. Go dance with one of these men." He coughed and winced. "They haven't sense enough to ask you."

"I just want to make sure you're taken care of."

Strong hands pulled her to her feet.

"Carmen, are you all right?" It was Don, his complexion pasty, worry etching lines on his face.

Anger forgotten, she leaned against him. "Why couldn't I have gotten here sooner? I should have gotten here in time."

He laid his arm across her shoulders. "Two hundred officers are asking themselves the same question. Just like me."

They moved aside to let the EMTs do their job. They stayed put until the Major was carried to a waiting ambulance.

She put her weapon back in her purse. "I'm going home."

"I'll take you."

"I'm a cop, Genonese." Brushing at her ruined dress, she tried to sound calm. "I'll get there on my own. Take care of the woman you brought."

"I take that as a no."

He gazed at her for a moment then nodded as if he'd been dismissed by a witch. She couldn't leave things in the mess they were in.

"Don, wait a minute." He turned to look at her, his dark eyes shadowed by his lashes. "This should teach us something."

"And, what would that be?"

"We can never be more than partners." She glanced down, not wanting him to see the pain in her eyes. "From now on, I'll keep my hands to myself, and you'll see me as just another cop."

"Sure." His deep voice stirred memories of sexy things he'd said to her in bed. "I got you loud and clear, Sergeant Redstone."

"Don't get hot under the collar, Genonese." Now she could speak her mind. He was pissing her off. "It might save us a lot of trouble in the future."

He loosened the knot in his tie. "I said I got your message. Shit."

Before she could do more damage to the situation, he turned around and headed back to the redhead in the green dress.

Carmen was too angry to let hurt feelings make her change her decision. He'd made it clear he wasn't going to attempt a decent explanation or make her reconsider.

She bit her lip to stop the rush of devastation twisting her heart.

Your damn level head and foolish rules have cost you everything.

Chapter Five

The next day started out like most, domestic disturbances and grocery store robberies. Carmen took a long drink of the Coke she'd left in the cruiser before making a stop at an apartment complex where a fight had broken out. The collar of her blouse hung in shreds with the top two buttons missing.

Don sat beside her, working his shoulders as if he were in pain. Maybe she should inquire about it. No, he'd just criticize her method of handling a drunk.

"Want a drink, Genoese?" She remembered he'd dropped his when they got to the family riot.

He took the cup and drank thirstily. "Thanks. Let's stop somewhere for another. I'm dry as dust."

"Okay." Damn her craven hide. She made sure to place her lips on the spot he'd had his. She'd always done that, and couldn't break the habit. The dash computer lit up, and she nodded in its direction. "Take that, will you? I have to find a pin for my blouse."

Don put down his clipboard and listened to the message. He took notes, grimacing as he wrote. "Now what? I have half a mind to apply for a spot with the FBI." He drank the last of her Coke. "I couldn't catch anymore shit than being with this crazy outfit."

"I heard." Whatever the problem at headquarters, it couldn't compare to the fact that Don really wanted to leave the department. That meant he would be leaving her as well. That wasn't supposed to matter to her, but God, it did. "It's probably nothing. You know how they call you in a dozen times if a felon gripes about you."

He gazed at her with those dark, sexy eyes and nodded. "You're probably right." In an unconscious gesture, he touched the riot gun bolted to the dash. "We'd better get downtown before they send out the dogs."

"Look in my purse and get my sewing kit." His look of surprise made her want to laugh, but she held it in. "Look for a safety pin."

"Damn." He grabbed her satchel and rummaged through the contents, finally holding up her emergency repair kit. He opened the plastic box and dug out a huge safety pin. "This okay?"

"It'll do." She pulled into a fast food parking lot and turned on the overhead light.

While she closed the blouse over her bruised breast, Don quietly observed her.

"You haven't said much about seeing the chief." He took the box from her and dropped it in her purse. "You're not worried about being pulled in for an ass chewing? Not even the least bit pissed off?"

"Nope." She drove from the parking lot and headed downtown.

Carmen couldn't afford any more problems with the department. She had no intentions of staying on the street or being a uniform until retirement. That wasn't good enough, especially since she'd worked so hard for advancement.

She knew Don had applied for captain when she had, almost a year ago. He was too good a cop to keep chasing two-bit drug dealers and the hassle of domestic calls.

Her thoughts drifted on a forbidden journey, teasing her with the memory of his lips on hers, the weight of his muscular body pushing her into the mattress. She had recurring wet dreams of him and was tempted to lure him back into her bed, but it would have to look like his idea.

"We should have gotten drinks back there." His bellyaching erased her erotic daydream. "And, I need to empty Big John."

"For God's sake, Don. You'll survive."

She found barking at him a release for her knotted up nerves. The closer they got to downtown headquarters, the tighter her nerves coiled. Keeping him ticked off meant he'd forget to insult her.

God, what was she in for now?

* * * *

Three months later, and she still treated him like shit. Don had thought he knew women, but Carmen showed him how little he knew.

"Did you come up with anything? This is a hell of a note, being dragged down here like a cut steer." He cleared his throat at her cool glance in his direction. "We went over that river bottom arrest."

So the brass got to live like this, drapes at the windows and flowers on a table? Redstone would fit perfectly in here, only she'd have buffalo robes covering the windows and a moose head on the wall. She caught him staring at her and broke the deafening silence with a not unexpected insult.

"You're paranoid, Don." She sounded confident, but the constant checking of time on her watch drove him crazy.

Sitting in the Chief's office wasn't on his list of great things to do.

And why had they both been called in at the same time?

Hell with that. He was more concerned with getting Carmen to pull some more time in the sack. He hadn't meant to hurt her, or do any of the lowdown things she thought he'd done. On the other hand, he wasn't ready to start explaining his every move to the woman who wanted nothing beyond a working relationship with him.

When Major Green had been shot, all he could think of was Carmen could have been the one lying on the floor. He'd been shaking so hard, he'd scared himself while driving that chick back to her apartment and now, he couldn't even remember her name.

Carmen. Beautiful, hot blooded, hot tempered Carmen Redstone. He didn't realize he had been grinning until she hissed at him.

"I'm glad you find this so amusing." She walked to the water cooler and filled one of those dinky little cups.

"By the way, Genonese, what have you done?"

He jumped up in a flash and crossed the room to grip her arm. "I could ask you the same question. You've run the string out on good behavior. Shot anyone in the ass lately?"

That drew fire. The slightly drawn lips and narrowed eyes told him she wanted to punch him.

"Get back in your cage, you bastard." She drank the water and death gripped the cup.

"Can't take it, huh?" He laughed and pried the paper from her clenched fist. "I don't have any idea why we're here but I'd suggest we act as a team, not good cop, bad cop."

"And we both know which you are."

"I was worried about you at the reception, Redstone." He'd never had to apologize for making a hare-brained mistake with a woman before. Forgetting he'd loosely made a date with that redhead had been the dumbest thing he'd done in years.

"Your brain's in your jeans." She slid by him and out of the corner he'd had her in for a few seconds. "Get this straight, Genonese, I don't give a damn about your personal life. It has nothing to do with me."

"What happened to us being friends?" Don knew that was a stretch, being friends with a wild cat, but something crazy in his blood made him want to be in her favor. "And, Miss Carmen, you've been in my jeans more than I have."

Her eyes narrowed in silent warning. He couldn't stop the grin that messed up his angry expression.

She was beautiful, and he especially liked the way her eyes changed colors to match her mood. Right now, they were jet black. Really pissed off Jet.

"Don."

"Yes, dear."

"Shut your mouth." She glanced over his shoulder. "Chief Drummond is here."

He straightened his attitude and turned to look at the burly man in a gray pinstripe suit. Hell, this scene could be straight out of *The Godfather*.

Chief Drummond waved his fat cigar in their direction and sat at his desk. "This won't take long." He dropped the cigar in a crystal ashtray and gestured toward the two chairs near the desk. "Now, you both have applied for the rank of captain some months back." He cocked an eyebrow at them as they took their seats. "There weren't any vacancies then."

Carmen glanced at him and gave the tiniest shrug he'd ever seen. Don figured she was getting set for another disappointment. What the hell had the Chief hauled them in for? To see the disgust on their faces at his denial of approval?

"We understand, sir." She started to stand, but the chief's wave sat her down again. "We all have to wait our turn. Sir."

Damn it. How could she go on being nice to the pompous prick? He probably planned to cut her to shreds.

"Sir, we appreciate your time in explaining the situation." Don leaned back in his chair, copping a nonchalant pose. "Is there another reason you made time for us today?"

The look he got from the busy man fried his nuts. Once again, he'd stepped over the line.

"Genonese, you have a reputation for having a fast tongue and faster trigger finger."

Aw, shit. Don couldn't argue with that, and now, he was chin deep in crap. "A reputation well deserved, sir. I spoke out of turn. Sorry."

Carmen slid an amused glance his way. She obviously enjoyed his being on the carpet. The air weighed a ton while he waited for the hammer to fall. He sucked in a deep breath when the Chief focused on pulling a folder from the desk drawer.

"Now, if I can get on to more serious matters." The head man of the department shot a warning look at Don. "Two of our best men have been promoted up the chain, and that leaves room for a couple of new captains. The board has decided the two of you, Sergeant Redstone and you, Sergeant have been given the promotions."

Don felt his tongue swell in his mouth. A promotion he'd given up on, and Carmen looking radiant even though she sat still as a rock.

"Thank you, sir." Don stood and reached across the desk to shake the chief's hand. "Oh, and thank the board for okaying these promotions."

With as little emotion as a person could pull off, the Chief went on with his little speech. "From now on, you'll have a squad of men to take care of and an ass load of paper work. Still want the job, Genonese?"

"Hell yes." Don grinned, not caring at the moment if he was the Chief's worst dream. "Sir."

What the hell, a guy could act a little goofy at a time like this. Carmen finally stood and shook hands with their boss, her face serene under the tension. What the hell was she feeling?

"Congratulations, Genonese." She headed for the door, leaving him to trail after her and that sexy whiff of perfume she always wore. "It's time for us to pull our shift. I'll drive, since you look hung over."

She didn't completely fool him with that calm demeanor. Her stride was quick, and she smoothed the hair at her nape before they stepped out in the steamy evening heat.

"Carmen." She turned to face him. He struggled to find the best way to humble himself without sounding like a wimp. "How about having a drink after our shift? Kind of a celebration?"

"No thanks."

Short and sweet, she chopped his dick off and handed it to him. He couldn't believe she saw him as a pariah after the blazing sex they'd had. The way she turned him down stunned him.

"I didn't ask to get in your pants, Redstone."

"Yes, you were." She got in the car and waited for him to get in. "I'm going to go see my mom after work."

Don eyed her with new insight. She took pride in the promotion after all. He hadn't even thought about his family or what they would say.

Luscious Carmen had a soft side to her stony exterior. It made her that much more beautiful.

As they drove to the latest drug bust, he wanted to rid himself of the mounting desire in his balls. How long could he be with her ten hours a day and not have a hard on all the time?

Carmen was like no other woman he'd met, sensual in every way. Even while she twisted some jerk's arm, she took his breath away.

Chapter Six

Carmen touched the handmade turquoise and silver squash blossom necklace her mother fastened around her neck. She'd wanted the piece of art since seeing it in the display case.

"Momma, this is too expensive to give away." Carmen protested mildly, thrilled to receive such a gift.

She loved her mother so much. Everything about her was perfect, right down to the heavy braid gracing her straight back. Years of abuse had not dampened her pride or joy of living.

"I have been saving it for you." Ruby Redstone was a woman of few words. New and unexpected ones hit like a bolt of lightning. "You're in love now, Carmen. Why are you so unhappy?"

"In love?" Carmen flushed with embarrassment. She never could hide her emotions from her only ally. "That's ridiculous, Momma. I'll let you know when I find the right man."

"Don't let your childhood ruin your chance for happiness." Ruby kissed her flustered daughter's cheek. "You should be celebrating your success, not wasting time with me." She picked up a half finished bracelet, smiling as she added some feminine advice. "A humming bird likes sweet flowers, dear. You have yet to blossom."

"Momma, what the heck does that mean?" Carmen knew what the wheedling comment meant. It meant she could bag Don with sweetness and femininity. "I only attract bumble bees, and they have a sting that reminds you to keep your petals closed."

They laughed with shared affection, each having known the crushing blow of rejection from a heavy handed man.

After having coffee and a look through the new items of Ruby's small, thriving jewelry boutique, Carmen headed home. She needed sleep to face another night with Don. She had to be on top of her game to keep him from proving she wasn't worthy of her coveted promotion.

Three blocks from her apartment, Carmen remembered her mother's shocking observation. *In love? It's not love when you're the only one feeling the emotion.*

A kernel of an idea settled in her brain. Maybe a cruise, or a couple weeks in the tropics would help her get over Genonese.

Of course, you'd cut it short and run right back to see if he's really as hot as you pictured.

Spotting a liquor store, she drove into the parking lot, intending to buy a six-pack or a case of soft drinks. Bottles of wine sparkled on the glass display shelves. She carried a soft Merlot to the counter along with the colas.

"Celebrating?" The older man smiled at her while bagging her items.

"No, just thirsty."

She went back to her car, groaning when she spotted two high school kids hanging around the trash dumpster, taking swigs from an open beer. She wouldn't hassle them tonight. Not too much. She drove up next to their shadowy party area and flashed her shield.

"You guys twenty-one?"

The beer bottle hit the concrete and shattered in the bag. "No ma'am. We wuz just going home."

"See that you do." She let the car ease forward a few feet. "I'll be back around, and if you're still here, you get a free ride in the paddy wagon."

"Yes, ma'am." The two skinny kids took off like deer, probably wetting their pants.

Carmen grinned when they looked back before turning the corner. *Little shits.*

At her apartment, she pulled her car into a parking space in the crappy lean-to garage, and got out, tired and ready to crawl into bed. Walking to the entrance, she recognized the car parked in front of the building.

Genonese.

She approached the maroon GMC wagon, and leaned on the fender. "The woman on the second floor will call the cops if you sit here too long."

He leaned across the seat, grinning in his special 'I want to fuck you' way. "Okay. Invite me in."

Invite him in? The arrogant bastard.

"Sure." *Admit it, Carmen. You're happy to see him.*

He didn't seem surprised by her quick agreement. He got out of his car and locked it before following her into the building.

She trembled with apprehension, afraid now of all the crazy feelings racing through her. Did he have to stand so close? Damn it, where was that light switch?

The door opened and they walked in, not speaking until he took the wine and coke from her hand. "Planning a party?"

"I will, as soon as you leave." She placed her purse and weapon on the coffee table. "Did you come back for your jeans?"

"I came back to celebrate with you, Captain Redstone." His fingers toyed with the heavy necklace between her breasts. "And, to tell you, I think they picked the right woman."

She moved away, carrying the drinks into the dark kitchen. Images of him and that woman iced her blood. His shadow fell over her when he walked into the room. "I think you'd better go celebrate with the redhead."

Damn, why did you let him in? You're a fool.

Her attempt to freeze him out melted under the touch of his hands on her waist. "Let's not go there, Carmen. This is between you and me."

"There's nothing between us, Don." She shivered when his lips teased her earlobe. "Why don't you leave?"

He ignored her suggestion and methodically removed the combs from her upswept hair.

"I've always wanted to do that." His hand locked in the long strands while he gazed at her with arousal flickering in his eyes.

Stay? Go? What should she do?

The heat building in her blood screamed with the desire to walk into his arms, yet the resentment of his lies blocked her emotions.

"Very poetic, Don, but I'd rather you didn't touch me."

He eased closer until he chin grazed her cheek. "Why not? Afraid you like me? Just a little."

Ah, heaven in blue jeans warmed her soul while he pressed soft kisses on her mouth. Like him? She loved him more than her next breath. Her heart pounded out the words she couldn't say.

"I'm not sure." Her protest had been faint, but clear to him. She eagerly gave in to the fire burning out of control in her body.

"I'm sure for both of us." He took his time removing the pin from her blouse and released the buttons. Her body tensed with high expectation at the touch of his firm lips on her bare breast. "It's been too long, Carmen…too long."

"Meaning?" Why couldn't she keep her mouth shut and simply enjoy the only man she wanted?

He didn't answer and pulled her close in his arms. "Not this time, Redstone. I know you want me as much as I want you. No more insults to ruin a perfect hard on."

With a few simple words, he lit the fuse to desire, and she gave in to the ache in her body. "Let's see what you call perfect."

She slowly unzipped his jeans, pushing her hand into his shorts to grip his cock in a firm hold. She shivered with pleasure at the weight of hot, rigid man in her possession. He covered her hand, groaning against her neck.

For several minutes, they stood in silence, blanketed in need and overwhelming pleasure of touching, his hands moved to her ass, holding her close.

She loved his mouth, her own opening to feel the plunder of his tongue. He tasted good, fresh and clean and just plain Don. He filled her senses to overflowing. Whatever made her think she could say no to him, to refuse the hot steam of wild sexual awareness moving from his hand into her pussy?

There was no use fighting how quickly she opened every door for him or how he easily vanquished her stubborn resistance. All her torment burned away, and she gave in to the throbbing need to be his woman.

Urgency made her hug his neck, holding his mouth to hers in a rough, searching kiss. She loved his fingertips grazing the mounds of her breast and his mouth pressing to her nipples. The gasp she had been tamping down escaped the moment he began to suck, and her nails dug deep in his back.

She helped him unzip her slacks, shuddering with pleasure, and straining to him while his fingers moved her panties aside to tug gently on her pubic hair. She liked it, his teasing way of driving her crazy. Her juices ran wild, and his fingers inched deep inside her until she was positive she felt them reach her soul.

In a wildfire to have him, she worked quickly to rid him of his shirt and unbuckled his jeans, not allowing his fingers leave her as his clothes fell to the floor.

He kicked his jeans aside while he held her still to stroke her clit, paying close attention to her breast she thrust toward him. She nearly collapsed with passion, longing to claim his hard cock in her throbbing pussy. To stop for a second was precious time lost.

"Fuck me now, Don." The demand had come out as a raspy whisper. "Now—right here."

Scorching heat rose up around them, burning away the days of loneliness and doubt Carmen had struggled through. Her man handled her like she weighed nothing, his mouth warm and devastatingly delicious.

"You wear too many fucking clothes." His soft complaint was muffled by the ripping sound of her blouse being torn off her body. "You didn't like that blouse anyway, did you?" He teased her, obviously not concerned about the shredded fabric he tossed on the floor.

He displayed real talent for working hooks of bras, freeing her breasts in one swift motion. "I'm glad you know I love that bra." She squeezed his dick, pulling firmly to make her meaning clear. "You're wearing shorts. I want you naked."

He shed the last bit of clothing he wore, and immediately pressed her to the wall. His mouth crushed down on hers, exploring every angle of her mouth, his tongue seeking hers in a deep, hot kiss.

They kissed with such passion, she sizzled from head to toe, her juices wetting her thighs. She held him in a grip she reserved for a badass trying to give her trouble, wanting the moment to never end.

He sucked her nipples until they ached with the need to swell, and his hands pulled her ass closer to his cock. His pre come lubed her belly as they moved slowly against each other.

She bucked her hips to let him know she was more than ready, and climbed his hard body as he lifted her leg up to his waist. They breathed hard, heat building to such intensity flashes of fire swirled around them. He teased her clit with the head of his dick, slowly pushing forward to fill that aching emptiness in her.

He braced her weight against the wall with his arm, holding back for a second before stroking in and out with a slow torturous rhythm.

She encouraged him to move faster by slapping his hard ass. His deep laugh aroused her desire to dangerous levels, and she slapped the rock hard muscles again.

"You too tired to screw tonight, Genonese?" He drove into her then, the pressure riveting against her tailbone. "Oh my God, that's what I want, damn you. Stop holding back or I'll finish myself."

Carmen gave in to every wave of ecstasy, moved with him, grinding her pussy as close to his cock as she could without throwing him to the floor. Her climax roared up and crashed at the point when she thought his dick touched her heart, splintering inside her with sweet, blissful agony.

His final thrust and loud groan ended the firestorm of pleasure. She was too tired to move and let him carry her to the couch.

"Damn, Redstone, we fucked like two minks, and I still want more." He dropped down to lay on her, pulling her nipple into his mouth.

For a crazy second, she thought about telling him she was too tired, but the orgasmic flicker in her pussy still yearned for more.

He was hard again, and she wouldn't let that wonderful thing go unrewarded. She closed her fingers around him, squeezing the head and working her hand back and forth. He wet her fingers with the perfect lube before settling in between her legs. His dick found her, and he crushed her lips beneath his, squeezing her breast as he pumped into her.

The second orgasm was better than the first. The third time he came sent her off into space.

"Captain Genonese, you've outdone yourself this time." She wanted to purr, lying in what she considered paradise with the man she most loved to irritate.

He lifted his head and smiled, his hair mussed just the way she liked it. "You never disappoint me, Captain Redstone." He kissed her, nibbling on her lips. "In fact, you're way too damn good for me."

"I pick my partners, Genonese, and don't forget it." Had she read something wrong into his comment? It didn't matter. She couldn't let him think he had control of their situation. "Will you get off me, or do I roll you?"

"Hey." He slid off her to the floor. His dark eyes flashed fire. "What the hell's wrong with you? Sometimes I think the only reason you give me ass is to humiliate me afterwards."

"Oh, shut up, you big baby." She stepped over him and stomped off to the bathroom. As she washed up, Carmen thought of a dozen ways to make up with him, but the devil won out.

He lay sprawled on the floor, eyes closed and fucking beautiful with no clothes on. He tried to catch her ankle as she walked by him on her way to the coffee table. She dug into her purse and pulled out her handcuffs. The metal felt cold in her hand, the silver bracelet snapping around his right wrist with no problem. He stared up at her in astonishment.

"What the hell are you doing, Redstone?"

"What's it look like, Captain?"

She snapped the open cuff to the fancy claw foot leg of the couch.

"That's not funny, Carmen." He sat up, reaching for her. "All this because of something you thought I said? Goddamn it!"

"Wrong as usual."

"Is this one of your payback tricks?"

"No, I do this to all my guys." She went into the bedroom and pulled on a t-shirt and jeans. Scuffing out to the living room, she picked up her purse. "I'm going to go have something to eat. I'll be back in a few minutes. Unless I decide to go shopping."

He glared at her, and her heart thumped with a raw excitement. For the first time, he was in her control, and she liked it.

"Carmen."

She went out the door, closing it and making unnecessary noise while pretending to lock it. Her power surge melted after only ten minutes. Maybe she'd better go back and make sure he was okay.

He shot a glare her way when she went back inside the apartment. "You still here?"

"When I get out of these, I'm going to teach you a lesson."

She sat down in front of him, touching his thigh, tracing the hard muscle up to his crotch. "Say nice things to me, Don."

He growled. "You're a bitch, Redstone."

"I already know that." She pulled her shirt over her head and dropped it on his face. "Tell me I'm pretty."

"Okay."

"No. Say it."

"You're pretty."

He eyed her breasts, and just that simple thing made her nipples hard. "Tell me how I make you crazy for sex just looking at me."

"You make me crazy for sex just thinking about you, Carmen."

"That sounded very convincing." She unzipped her jeans. "I'm going to do something to you, Don." She kicked her jeans off. "Don't move and you won't feel a thing."

"Okay, but don't bite my dick, baby." His glare had become a hot lick that urged her on in their sex game.

She wasn't surprised that he had a hard on, his voice always told her when he was aroused. His flat stomach jerked under her hand and his cock flattened to his belly in an amazing stretch.

Fitting her mouth over the head, she ran her tongue around the smooth tip, exploring his length. He was in her mouth, hard and veined as she took him in as far as she could. She sucked, and he groaned, his free hand in her hair. He didn't pull her head closer, just gritted his teeth and moaned.

She licked his length and scraped her teeth up to his balls, mouthing them on her way back down. He was pulsing, his grip in her hair urging her to bring him to climax.

She leaned forward and took him deep in her throat, pulling the head of his dick with hard, steady suction. She didn't back off when he came, his hips lifting to get closer to her. She could be addicted to the salty, perfumed taste of him, the sound of his voice saying she took him to heaven. He fell back on the floor and groaned with resignation. She tingled with the knowledge she'd whipped him into submission.

He didn't move while she opened the cuffs, just caught her around the waist to pull her down on top of him.

"You make me crazy for sex just thinking about you, Carmen."

"I'll use the cuffs more often."

While he dozed, she began to regret her crazy trick. The truth was she'd always wanted him to say those things to her. And she'd had to force the words out of him. Her free spirit tumbled to the ground.

Will you ever learn, Carmen?

Chapter Seven

Carmen listened to the little noises Don made while he got ready to leave the next morning. He was trying to be quiet, but his efforts were unsuccessful.

He sat on the edge of the bed to put on his shoes and leaned over to kiss her. "See you later, Sleeping Beauty."

She sighed, aching to pull him back into bed with her.

Why start something she would regret later? What in the hell would they say to each other? See you after work honey? What do you want for dinner?

That kind of conversation was reserved for normal people, not a loosely connected pair like them.

She sat up and tried to work the tangles from her hair. Lord, she looked a mess, from her whisker-burned chin to her aching thighs. What had made her think she had become a gymnast?

Grabbing Don's pillow, she pressed it to her face, inhaling his clean scent. At least he'd left her that.

She dropped it when her phone rang. The CID on the list irked Carmen.

"Captain Redstone?"

That was her. "Yes. This is Captain Redstone."

"I'm Ms. Grimly with KCPD personnel." The rustle of paper followed her monotone words. "You need to come into the office for information about your reassignment." Again, the crackle of paper preceded the rest of Ms. Grimly's words. "Also, you are required to fill out new forms for taxation and retirement funds due to your advanced rank."

Carmen followed the woman's drift, freshly aware of the possible mess she'd made of her life.

The conversation had been brief and mind numbing.

This day had to come, and her routine world had already turned upside down. This meant a new precinct, new people, and no partner.

She had to be downtown at eleven-thirty, just in time for lunchtime traffic. Why the hell had she wanted to advance in rank?

After a shower Carmen dressed in a navy blue pants suit and white cap-sleeved blouse, then pulled on a pair of black high heeled granny boots. No use going prim at this point. She omitted perfume, not wanting to offend any delicate noses.

Damn, she loved her perfume.

She'd been right. Traffic was a bear, and she already ran ten minutes late for the meeting. That should impress the brass. She drove into the underground garage and parked near the entrance. Maybe she wouldn't catch too much flak if she hurried. Too hot to worry about fashion, she shrugged off her jacket on her way to the bank of elevators and carried it over her arm.

The elevator to the third floor looked like a can of sardines, packed with plainclothes and uniformed officers. They all gave her the once over, the best looking one of the group tried his hand at flirting.

"That's a fine looking weapon on your hip."

She didn't comment, settled for staring at him with deadpan expression.

"Want to go to the firing range?" He leaned closer to murmur. "I can make a gun do things you never thought they could do."

She couldn't hold her tongue. The jerk pissed her off. "The name's Captain Redstone." She elbowed his ribs. "I wouldn't want to embarrass you."

Thank God the elevator stopped, and the doors opened. She got out and hurried to room 301. Her luck held. Several more officers walked in behind her. The receptionist smiled and checked their names off a list she had on a legal pad.

"Go right in." She sipped her coffee. "You're the last ones."

Oh shit. That meant the wheels were waiting and that meant an ass chewing. She stiffened her spine and walked in with the others.

The faces were a blur, all except that of Chief Drummond. He looked around at the group and sat at the head of the table. She slid into the nearest chair and waited for thunder to roll. To her relief, he started taking without the expected reprimand about being on time.

Carmen relaxed and glanced around the big table. She didn't know any of them on a friendly basis, and of course the wiseass from the elevator had come in behind her. She looked away when he winked at her. Just what she needed at a time like this.

She tried to concentrate on the Chief's words as he greeted all the new officers and froze when he said her name. He told the group about her outstanding record and something about her being a credit to the department. Her reply came out well in spite of her nervous tension.

"Thank you, sir." Had he complimented her, or called her a drooling idiot? She couldn't remember. The next name he mentioned changed everything.

"Don Genonese." Had there been a hint of humor in the Chief's voice as he gave a short synopsis of Don's career? Damn, she didn't know he'd been decorated three times for bravery in the line of duty.

She dared a quick glance at the group of officers standing at the back of the room.

Her heart flipped when Don nodded and winked at her. He was a lot of things, but he would never be a conformist.

God, he was the reason her heart banged against her ribs and made her feel giddy as hell. She looked away to find the flirt from the elevator gazing at her.

The rule of fraternization being discouraged fast forwarded through her brain. He was probably with IA.

Fast and Easy 57

Her attention jerked back to serious things coming fast and furious. Sign the damn promotion papers and see where she would be assigned.

Her hand faltered for a half second, holding the pen up while she took in all the changes coming in her life.

Captain Redstone is being sent to east patrol, will assume responsibility for forty men, and take over the evening shift. Well, hell. This was what she'd broke her back for, and wasn't she ready to be given more responsibility?

She unconsciously bit her lower lip and scrawled her signature on the form.

The secretary gathered up the forms and told the group to help themselves to the coffee and sweet rolls. Not interested in the mini-breakfast, she gathered her things to leave.

Her cell phone chimed in her purse, and Carmen hurried to silence the soft ring. She worried her mother might need her. She turned her back to the group and answered the call. "Redstone here."

"You're pretty."

"What?"

"And you make me hot just to look at you."

Her gaze slid to the back of the room. She should have been ticked off, but found Genonese's grin positively devastating. His voice crooned low, but she heard every word.

Stay calm, Carmen. He's playing with you.

His timing couldn't be more deplorable, but she loved his unorthodox moment of playfulness. Before she could think of a scalding comeback, the flirt wearing a flashy tie approached her. She closed her cell phone and dropped it in her purse.

"I don't need any of your sexist comments, buddy." She glanced back at Don, but he had already been caught up in conversation with another officer. It seemed the perfect time to escape the stifling scene.

"I'm Detective Bill Gentry." He handed her the jacket she'd left on her chair. "We'll be working together at East patrol."

"That's nice." Carmen clenched her teeth. If he represented the typical man she'd deal with every day on her new job, her life was going to be crap. "I'll see you there."

"If you need anything, just whistle."

"I'll do that, thanks." Might as well be civil to the jerk since she would be seeing him everyday.

* * * *

Don knew Gentry and his phenomenal luck with chicks. The bastard got more tail than a rock star. And now, he was trying to make a move on Carmen. A smirk worked its way over his mouth. She was too smart for Gentry's type, and her reaction hadn't been encouraging.

Hot waves of reality rocked him back on his heels.

Jealous? Worried? Feeling abandoned?

All that and more, plus the empty feeling of real loss knotted his gut.

What chance did he have with her now? Separated by a whole city from now on, they would be too busy for much spontaneous combustion sex.

Damn. Another reason to forget being with her cropped up in his mind. Stella, the redhead from East patrol. Hot, and always available.

He may as well crawl in a hole and pull it in after him as far as his Carmen was concerned. Yeah, he'd started to think of her as his woman. How bad was that?

He watched her walk to the door, Gentry hot on her heels. A pleasure rush hit him when Carmen turned and gave him a tiny tilt of her head, her signal to meet her outside the door.

Don ran into a chair and the snack table on his way out of that damn room.

He looked around the hallway, and finally spotted her near the back entrance.

God, she's beautiful.

"Hey." He stood as close to her as decently possible, bracing his hand on the wall. "I meant what I said, Carm."

Her fantastic brown eyes returned his gaze, and he swallowed his fear.

"Why didn't you wake me up before you left?"

The tingle of worry hit his gut again.

"You looked so sweet and comfortable. I didn't want to mess that up."

"You didn't want to mess with me, period."

He exhaled roughly. She wanted to fight.

"I thought we messed with each other plenty last night." He glanced over his shoulder. "Want to come over to my apartment after our shift?"

She touched the collar of his shirt and tugged on the starched material. "I have to go over the personnel roster and figure out who's who at East patrol."

"That will take you all of fifteen minutes." Had he heard softness in her voice? "I don't have to be at South patrol until the dog watch."

"Did you ask for that shift?" Her lips parted, and a sweet sigh spilled over them. "Okay. I'll stop by your place after I make my appearance at the station."

"I'll be waiting." He forgot to worry, her soft attitude lighting a blaze in his balls. He wanted to kiss her so bad his lips hurt. "See you, babe."

Pretending they weren't lovers took a hell of an effort. Watching her walk into the elevator with Gentry cut to the quick, and he didn't like it.

He'd never been jealous in his life, and the emotion stunned him.

Chapter Eight

Carmen tried to ignore the cold knot of dread in her stomach. East patrol was set up in a smaller building than the downtown precinct. The area was small, but the welfare of the officers there would rest on her shoulders.

Once inside the station, she looked around for what she thought might be the Captain's office. Ill at ease and ready to bolt for the door, she was stopped by a friendly voice.

"Can I help you, ma'am?" The officer smiled, waiting patiently to help her.

She relaxed immediately. "I'm Captain Redstone." She shook his hand. "Right now, Sergeant Rosen, I need to find my office."

He grinned and shook his head. "It's about time they sent a captain over here. Lewiston retired three months ago." He lay down the clipboard he'd been carrying. "You may have to redecorate in there." He led her to a small office at the rear of the building.

He'd been right. The room was cluttered with newspapers, magazines and a cracked coffee mug. She did a visual sweep, mentally rearranging the furniture and making a list of things to bring in.

"It's perfect, Sergeant Rosen." Carmen checked out the desk drawers. "Thank you for your help. I appreciate it."

"Anything you need, Captain, I'll see you get it." He looked at his watch. "The next shift will be here soon. I'll give you a roster to get you started."

She nodded, apprehension building again. "I'll need all the files Captain Lewiston was working on when he left." He started to leave,

Fast and Easy 61

but she stopped him. "Thanks again." She laughed softly. "And, would you point me in the direction of the conference room?"

He picked up the cracked coffee mug and inclined his head toward the door. "It's the first door to your left after you come in the lobby."

Carmen used one of the folded newspapers to squash a spider that crawled across the desk. "When the next shift arrives, I'll be there."

He left before she could ask another silly question.

She looked around for a mirror, but the former occupant had not been a vain man. Grabbing her purse, she found a small compact and lipstick.

Her hand shook, but she got the lipstick on her lips, not on her chin.

What the hell are you scared of, Carmen? You're all cops here.

For a few minutes, she gathered up magazines and papers, dumping them all in the old green tin waste basket. She tested the cracked leather desk chair. It squeaked in protest.

Her gaze wandered to the pebble glass window on the door. Replacing Captain Lewiston's name with hers was next on her agenda.

Voices coming from out front alerted Carmen that the new shift had arrived.

She shrugged into her jacket and took a deep, steadying breath.

Time to meet the troops.

They were like all cops she'd known, rowdy and loud as they greeted each other. Their mood eased her concern, and she walked into the conference room behind Sergeant Rosen.

"All right, men." He held his hands up to quiet the group. "We have our new Captain. I don't want Captain Redstone to think you're all a bunch of animals."

His comment drew a laugh out of the men and then Sergeant Rosen got down to the business at hand. While he read the latest list and information on felons they were to be on the lookout for, Carmen scanned the faces of the patrolmen.

Some of them were familiar. One face stood out.

The redhead.

Fury stomped her professional attitude to the floor.

She gripped her anger in a tight hold and smiled when the sergeant gestured for her to take over.

Her mouth was dry, and her legs were like limp spaghetti, but she managed to brace herself against the small podium.

"It will take a few days before I put names to faces." Her gaze shot to the redhead, nonchalantly slathering on a fresh layer of lipstick. "I want you to know from the start, if you have problems, ideas or suggestions for improving how the precinct could operate more efficiently, I'm ready to listen."

The redhead glanced around and then grinned. "I'll show you where Captain Lewiston's office is."

So, the bitch was a wise cracking bimbo too.

"That's my office now, and you'll learn that I'll rarely be in it." Carmen leaned forward over the mic. "I'm going to be in a car just like you. I'll be out in the field to see that procedures are followed." She almost bit her lip. "Do you have any questions?"

"Patrolman Stella Wells." The sergeant's gruff whisper gave away his irritation.

Carmen nodded. "Is there anything else, Wells?"

The redhead's response was a bored glance in her direction. She'd already pulled out an emery board and filed her nails.

That was too much for Carmen. "Patrolman Wells."

The bitch had the gall to glance around as if she'd heard incorrectly. The smart-assed smile on her face matched her disrespectful mouth. "Were you speaking to me?"

Hold your temper Carmen.

"I'd prefer you filed your claws off duty."

Stella stared back at her with cold green eyes. "Yes, sir."

"That's Captain Redstone." Carmen gripped her jacket in suppressed anger.

She heard muffled laughter. The men obviously enjoyed the exchange. She hadn't.

"That's all I have for now, men." Carmen breathed in a reviving breath, glad to turn the meeting back over to Rosen.

She would have felt much better if she'd been able to step on Wells' toes a lot more. Hell, there would be time for that later.

That wouldn't be enough to blot out the dizzying emotions threatening to ruin her life. Hurt? Damn right. Most of all, she was crushed that the love of her life wasn't committed to their relationship enough to tell her the whole truth about his life.

He had a lot of explaining to do. Her heart thudded its pain.

Then again, did she really want to hear it?

* * * *

Don hurried around his apartment, scooping up dirty clothes and throwing them in the bedroom closet. The dirty dishes that he'd neglected for several days were quickly hidden in the dishwasher.

He promised himself to keep his place cleaner since he never knew when she would come by. Carmen was coming. His heart beat faster at the thought she'd soon be here, in his arms and in his bed.

Where were those clean sheets?

He wasn't bothered that the sheets didn't match. He stood back to admire his handy work after getting them on his king-sized bed.

He hadn't had a woman in his apartment for a long time. He shook his head, realizing he'd been waiting for Carmen to stop hating him.

She'd want coffee or maybe some wine. Damn the luck, all his glasses were in the dishwasher. He grabbed two out of the jumble of dishes and was in the middle of washing them when the door bell chimed.

She had arrived. Turning the glasses upside down on the counter, he hurried to let her in.

"Carmen." His emotions shot back and forth from zany pleasure to mind-drugging desire. "Come in."

She was so hot, his body tensed like a loaded bear trap. How had he been the lucky bastard to have a woman like her?

He held out his hand to take her purse and jacket, but she'd have none of it. She jerked her arm away when he tried to pull her to him.

"Why didn't you tell me the redhead was a cop?"

"Aw, fuck." He groaned, knowing he had lied his way into knee deep shit.

"Yes, exactly what I wanted to talk about."

"What about her?" Once again, his dick had gotten him in trouble. This time, it mattered.

"I don't know anything about her." Carmen gazed at him in her cool steady way, not flinching, nowhere near tears. "Talk."

He wanted to lie, to deny knowing Stella Wells. That wouldn't work. He had to be honest. That's all Carmen would accept.

"Stella has been transferred through every precinct in Kansas City."

"And?"

"She wants to make rank and being friendly is her way of advancing."

"And did she?"

He thought Carmen would backhand him, but she only stood her ground, waiting for him to tell it all.

"She's fucked her way up the ranks and back down."

"How about Captain Genonese?"

"Yeah." That was a real fuck up. She wanted facts and exactly how it felt. Damn it. "A long time ago."

"You're sugar coating it, Genonese."

He couldn't keep his eyes off her breasts which heaved with anger.

"It couldn't have too long ago, or she wouldn't have been humping your leg at the Major's retirement party!"

"I wasn't with her." His blood pressure built to the point of real anger. "Her date went to the john before you showed up." Her fine brows shot up, and that meant she wanted more. "You turned me down as I recall. Said you were busy."

She headed for the door. "I'm not second best to anyone, Don." She slapped her jacket against the door. "May I assume you were there with someone else?"

"You may, but you're wrong." She wasn't going to listen, and he was tired of defending himself. "I only went after the Major more or less insisted I show up. That's it."

"Okay." She opened the door. "I'll see what I can do about moving Wells to your new precinct. She's not what I want on the streets of my area."

"Carmen." He yelled after her as she ran from his apartment. "Yeah, you do that. At least she doesn't rip my ass every time I see her. Goddamn it."

Chapter Nine

Carmen rested her head in her hands and rubbed her temples. The headache she had all day refused to go away. The paper work seemed to never end. Officer reports were sometimes illegible, and she hated calling them in to clarify things they had written.

Until she learned to decipher their handwriting, she'd struggle through and okay their reports. All that added to the mountain of duties, plus town council meetings and court dates. She spent any spare time left in the day learning all she could about East patrol and the officers assigned there.

Every one of them was a good, solid cop, all except Stella Wells. Like a fly, she never lit in one spot long enough to access her value. She'd been given several reprimands for being late and also insubordination.

In an attempt to find a fatal flaw in the woman's character, Carmen read Stella's file several more times.

She leaned back in the new, padded chair pilfered from an empty office and thought over her burning quest to dislike and drum Patrolman Wells out of the department.

Why the hell are you so jealous of her? You're the one that kicked Genonese loose. You screwed up again.

She jumped with surprise at a noisy rapping on her door. "Yes. Come in."

"Hey, Captain." Detective Bill Gentry stood tall and self-assured in the doorway. "There's a standoff down at the Saigon Food Mart."

Damn. The second basket case that afternoon.

Carmen rose and clipped her weapon to the waistband of her slacks. She grabbed her light uniform jacket, shrugging into it while contacting the field Sergeant on the scene.

The night was going to be hell. While she was getting her equipment, her computer ticked off news of a major crash near the casino. There were several fatalities. She couldn't be both places at once, no matter how badly she wanted to.

"I'm on my way, Thomas." The patrolman described the situation as critical. The doped up guy causing all the hell was armed and wanted for murder. "Shots have been fired, and the kid held hostage is twelve."

Twelve. The boy must be terrified.

Gentry's ever present grin vanished. "Let's roll."

"I'll take my car." At his look of surprise, she offered a good reason for her decision. "If this is cleaned up quickly, I'm heading out to the emergency on 291."

He nodded. "Good call." He got in his car and took the lead toward the Market district.

Carmen followed him out of the parking lot, hitting the lights and rehashing in her mind all the training she'd had in hostage situations.

No all out assault would do in this instance. A boy's life hung in the balance, and she couldn't even go in after the bastard holding him. That was left to the patrolman. Damn. This job wasn't anything more than being a room mother. She didn't like it.

The dash computer lit up, and several messages tracked across the monitor. More news on the six car pileup on 291. She was needed there too. Message two described a male in black sagging shorts and a black hockey shirt prowling back alleys in the River Quay area.

Carmen's heart turned upside down in her chest.

That was the area where her mother lived.

Don't go down there, Carmen. They won't let you go in.

She couldn't help herself. Using her quick call list on her cell phone, she broke all the rules once again.

"Don."

"My Carmen?"

She warmed at his soft greeting. "Are you in the River Quay area?"

"Just pulled up in front of your momma's house."

Carmen heard the door of his cruiser open and close. "How's it look around there?" He didn't respond and she panicked. "Genonese?"

He answered at last. "The dogs found him, Carm. A ten-year-old picking up beer cans to trade for cash."

She could hardly breathe, wanted to tell him how much she loved him right then and there, but that bullshit was over between them.

"Thanks, Genonese." She gripped the steering wheel to hold back the sweet sentiment drumming on her tongue. "I'm on my way to the hostage situation downtown. Are there enough officers handling the 291 pile up?"

His rich voice came back with a soft laugh. "I'm heading there now."

Why the hell was she holding the cell phone open? They were through talking. Weren't they? "Thanks again."

"Carm."

"Yes?"

"I miss you."

"Same here, Genonese."

She heard his cruiser door slam and the siren broke the silence. He was going one direction, and she was going another. That was how it would be from now on.

Reality smacked her hard in the face. It hurt.

You wanted it this way. Didn't you?

Flashing lights and barking dogs at the standoff scene snapped Carmen out of her thoughts of Don into a professional desire to resolve the situation with no one getting hurt.

She jumped out of her car and ran to the group of patrolmen near the market's entrance. She located Patrolman Thomas.

"Has anyone talked with the perp? What's his beef?"

The young cop pointed to a thin woman wringing her hands and weeping uncontrollably. "That's his girlfriend. She says she broke it off with him after he choked her this morning."

"He wants her back?" Carmen's back hurt from the tensing of her muscles. She couldn't stop the ugly memories that crept into her thoughts. She knew too much about psycho men in love. "Have you given her a bull horn to settle him down with some sweet talk?"

"Not yet, ma'am."

"Well, do it. Now." She walked toward the line of men guarding the building front. "Is the boy a relative of his?"

Gentry appeared at her side and read his notes from a small tablet. "The kid's a bus boy in the restaurant. No kin. Just unlucky."

The frightened woman pleaded with her ex-boyfriend to release the boy and come out. The bull horn was heavy and it wobbled as she held it in both hands.

The noise around her would do nothing to settle the problem. The guy probably thought he would be shot if he stuck his head out.

Carmen moved away to yell at the K-9 cops. "Quiet your dogs but stay close. We may need to send them in for a search if this guy decides to hide."

"Affirmative, Captain." The Sergeant led his dog to his patrol car.

She worked her way to the front line where a mop of red hair caught Carmen's attention.

Stella Wells stood with her hand on the butt of her revolver, gaze fastened on the market entrance. She didn't look like a smart ass strumpet now, just a cop on full alert.

The radio on Carmen's shoulder buzzed crazily for a second before Thomas's calm voice came through.

"He's let the juvenile go but he isn't coming out."

She waited a split second before making her decision. "Get the dogs in there." She quickly added more instruction. "Double the uniforms in the back."

Sending men and dogs after someone was a last resort. The officers were in danger, and the dogs wouldn't quit until they found the man. She could hear the animals barking as they headed for the entrance, but they stopped the moment they were inside the building.

The boy had run out into the arms of Wells. The scene was touching. Stella gave him bottled water and talked to the boy as if she knew him.

Carmen walked around the line of officers to speak with the wide-eyed boy and the woman still holding the bull horn. "Are you okay?" He nodded and stared up at the second floor windows. "Officer Wells will ask you some questions about what happened and contact your parents. Are you up to it?"

Some of the fright had gone from his face, but his voice shook as he spoke. "He said he didn't want to hurt me, just use me to get his woman here."

What went through Carmen's mind wasn't fit for the boy to hear. The fool was going to leave the outcome to whatever the woman did. From where Carmen stood, she could see dark purple underling the woman's eyes and marks on her arms that looked suspiciously like cigarette burns.

Listening to the woman's pleas for her brutish boyfriend to come out irked Carmen. She swallowed her hot resentment and picked her words. "You're parents are coming this way. You can stand with them if you want to."

He ran off before Carmen could say more. A tiny twist of yearning to run away from the scene bothered her. That feeling vanished when the sound of gunfire echoed from inside the building.

Pulse racing and body tense, Carmen hurried to where the sergeant had taken cover near the entrance. "What the hell

Fast and Easy

happened?" She couldn't keep the anger from her words. "Give me your radio."

He unclipped the small radio from his collar and handed it to her. "We're not sure who fired the shots, ma'am." She didn't care that he was forced to follow her like a dog on a leash as she moved for a better view of the door. "What's the K-9 officer's name?"

Wincing as she tugged him forward, the sergeant answered quickly. "Patrolman Jenkins, ma'am."

Carmen gripped the radio in her clenched fingers. "Officer Jenkins, who fired those weapons?" She scowled at the delay of his response. "Jenkins."

The crackle of Jenkins radio was music in her ear. "I fired the weapon, Captain. The guy threw down on me and I had no choice."

"Is he alive?" Carmen tugged the sergeant several more steps. "The EMTs are coming up."

"He's alive and still screaming for his woman."

Carmen heard the dogs raising hell and the yowling demands from the wounded man.

She'd never been nearer vomiting on the job than at that moment. Stress dried her mouth out and twisted her gut into knots.

Hell and damnation. What happened to people when the weather got hot and sultry?

Something was wrong with her. She actual felt relief when Bill Gentry came to stand beside her. His grin was a little crooked as he wrote in his notebook.

"Damn good job of handling things, Redstone." He dropped the notebook in his jacket pocket. "I'd ride with you anytime."

"Thanks, Gentry."

She appreciated his comment, but she still had the unquenchable yearning to be out in the night with Don Genonese.

Chapter Ten

Sunday night, lonelier than she'd ever been, Carmen dressed in an ankle-length red floral silk skirt topped with a scoop neck white Tee-shirt.

She wasn't going for glamour. September was setting records for heat, and she was only interested in comfort.

Going to a bar where cops hung out said a lot about her life. She didn't have one. Not really. At least no one would give her shit there, and she didn't need some clown trying to pick her up.

She laughed under her breath. No one wanted to mess with the girl who'd shot Genonese in the ass.

That was probably a good thing, since she wasn't in the mood to explain to a masher she was already taken.

She fastened the single braid she'd made of her long hair and sighed with disgust. So much for looking entrancing for the boys. Eight o'clock and the bar should be filled with people looking for a place to unwind. She was one of them.

Several blocks from her apartment, Carmen thought about turning her car around and going home.

No, you have to stop holing up like a hermit.

She considered going to one of the downtown movie theaters, but scoffed at the idea. In her opinion, there hadn't been a good movie made in years. She wouldn't waste the money.

Before she could change her mind, she reached the bar.

As expected, The Shot was packed, and she had to park a block away.

A wolf whistle from a passing car was lost on her. Carmen hurried, giving the pair of men leaving the establishment a wide berth. They gave her appreciative smiles, the youngest stopping to attempt conversation.

"Hey, slim." He pointed to his companion. "Me and Greg would love to buy you a drink."

"No thanks."

He rocked back on his heels.

"I'm meeting someone." Carmen hurried on, glad to find the doors of The Shot standing open. The place must have lost its air conditioning for the owner to do that. Just great.

The lights were low, and she practically had to feel her way to the end of the old-fashioned oak bar.

"What can I get you, Redstone?" The bartenders smiling greeting gave her a sense of belonging. She'd frequented the place a lot in the beginning of her so-called career. It had been the place to go, until she'd partnered up with Genonese. After the incident, she stopped going. Damn, that man had always been a boil on her ass.

She glanced at the bottles behind the bar, trying to think of something that wasn't too deadly. "Vodka and orange juice with lots of ice."

Music from the jukebox played too loudly, and several couples moved toward the small dance floor. Carmen paid for her drink and sipped slowly, leaning against the bar to check out the crowd.

She didn't look up when someone moved into the space beside her. It was crazy, but the scent of a special aftershave overcame the dozen different smells drifting around her.

There was no mistaking the voice that melted her heart.

"Come here often, pretty lady?"

Carmen sipped her drink, praying her legs would hold her up. "Not often." She worked her tongue in her mouth, fearing the thing had frozen solid. "How about you?"

Don made her weak with emotions too wild to keep at bay, reducing her to a quivering idiot. He took a long drink of the beer he'd ordered.

He stood so near his arm brushed hers. His voice was low as he delivered a bullet to her soul. "Not since I lost my girl."

Damn the tear that threatened to spill down her cheek. She knew him well enough to note the bullshit in his words. But, god she wanted to believe him.

"So, what did you do to lose your girl?"

"I don't really know." He curled his fingers around her braid, moving his hand down to her waist. "I want her back."

What was he saying? That he wanted her for tonight or forever?

He wasn't smiling his sexy, come-on-baby smile. His gaze held hers in soft seduction.

Taking her hand to swing it gently, he placed her arm around his waist.

The music changed from rock to a love song. She followed him to the dance floor, going into his arms without resistance. What could it hurt?

More than you can handle if you don't freeze him out.

They didn't dance, but clung to each other, the beat of their hearts one sweet rhythm. Her blood sang with joy at being in his arms with the warmth of his body pressed to hers.

She loved him so much it hurt.

"Carm." He whispered against her burning ear. "You're pretty. I get hot just thinking about you."

She pressed her cheek to his broad chest and smiled at his comment. "I had to pull a forty-five on you to hear that the first time."

"No need for that, Carmen." His lips touched the corner of her mouth. "I miss being with you. Life's gone to hell since we've been apart."

The thing she'd avoided happened without summoning it from its hiding place. Desire overtook her mind and body. She lifted her arms to encircle his neck and pressed her lips to the fast beating pulse under his ear.

She melted into him, drinking in his clean scent, reacquainting her senses to the hard frame of his body. Carmen knew it would never be enough.

Just like the first time, she had no resistance and she didn't care.

She'd found heaven and couldn't tear herself away.

Being bumped by another couple didn't bother her. She didn't want to ever leave, not until Don broke the misty spell.

"Want to go talk?" He squeezed her tight, his voice deep and smooth. "How about my place?"

"Yes." She didn't have to repeat her answer. He quickly captured her hand in his and led her from the dance floor, walking fast and ignoring the calls from his buddies at the bar to stay and have a drink. "Do you want to stay for a while?"

He didn't speak until they were out in the sultry night air, and his arms were around her. "Are you kidding? I thought about not coming tonight. But, damn I'm glad I did."

She knew she was breathing because her heart was pounding and sent her blood pressure off the scale.

He opened the door to his GMC wagon, helping her in before running to the driver's side to jump in beside her.

She tried to match his calm attitude, but the effort was useless against weeks of hungering to be with him. Don draped his arm across her shoulders while he drove, but kept his eyes on traffic. His self-control drove her crazy, no fast hands in a rush, no wise cracks or suggestive remarks.

After what seemed like hours of torture, he parked in front of his apartment building.

She stayed put while he got out and came around to help her from the car, surprising her when he picked her up to carry her to the entrance.

"I didn't get a chance to tell you before, but you're a damn good looking woman, Carm." He set her down and opened the heavy door, letting her walk in first.

Carmen wasn't accustomed to sweet talk from him. She liked it, but felt a little embarrassed at such flowery prose coming from the toughest cop in Kansas City.

Inside his apartment, the air hung heavy with apprehension and her growing desire to touch him.

He made it easy for her, taking her purse to drop it on the floor. She was glad he didn't turn on the lights so he couldn't see the blaze of passion in her eyes. So far, she seemed to be the only one being consumed by flames of desire.

He stood near a small credenza, emptying his pockets when she decided it had been long enough.

"Don." Her fingers shook and her legs weakened, but she had already stepped out of her skirt when he turned to look at her. "Enough conversation. I haven't waited all this time to hear what you think of the weather." She took several steps toward him. "I want you Copper, and if you don't feel the same, tell me right now."

* * * *

Want her! How many wet dreams had he awoke from, sporting a massive hard on because she'd been riding him like a jackhammer on fire?

"I feel the same, Carm." He gazed at her for a moment before pulling his shirt off over his head. "You have no idea how much I want you."

He'd left the bathroom light on in his hurry to leave, and the light bathed her golden skin in its warm glow. Just being close to her, he had a hell of a time keeping his balls under control.

He touched the gleaming squash blossom necklace nestled between her breasts. She was perfection with beads of passion sweat glistening on her smooth flesh. He moved his hands carefully, freeing her long hair from the braid to drape around her shoulders and breasts.

She trembled, standing still while her nipples peaked under his palms. His cock tried to claw its way through his jeans, an erection he wanted to share with her.

His reserve fled on clumsy feet when she licked her lips and began unbuckling his belt.

"You have on too many clothes, Genonese." The brush of her fingers on his belly sent his muscles into spasms. "I want to see your body. I want to lick your nipples and everything else."

He couldn't play the pussy any longer. Raw need canceled out his carefully plotted approach.

"You can see and lick anything you want, baby." He pulled her against his throbbing dick, held her face in his hands to cover her mouth in a hungry kiss. His knees were weak from the taste of her lips and tongue that played with his. Her teeth tugged on his lip in urgent demand for sex, and he wasn't about to make her wait. He knew firsthand her ability to take him out like a rank armature when she wanted action.

He caught her hand when she worked his stiff dick into a jerking frenzy. The sultry laugh he loved spilled from her lips while he tore her panties off her lush body. He ran his palm down her stomach to brush the soft hair framing her pussy. She was wet, and the scent of her arousal grabbed him by the balls.

"My bra, Don?" She held his cock in a firm grip, her soft gaze following the movement of his hands while he unhooked the front-closed bra.

"My God." His soft comment expressed everything he felt as he eyed the full mounds of her breasts. She looked exquisite, ripe and his. "I want you, Carmen Redstone."

Her strong fingers cupped his balls, the sensation fanning the flames of desire to fuck her. He groaned when she spread her legs, making it easier for him to dip his fingers inside her. She gripped his thigh with her leg, moving her hips against his fingers, groaning in erotic pleasure.

He lifted her higher on his thigh, reveling in her soft breasts against his heaving chest, and her sweet tasting tongue plunging deep inside his mouth. Her lips were full and pliant, forming to his in a scorching demand for fulfillment.

For the second time that night, he picked Carmen up to carry her, the warmth of her body matching his own as he took her to his bed. He laid her on the quilt, quickly removing his jeans before joining her.

He moved to settle in between her open legs, trailing kisses up her thigh to her pussy. Her legs jerked and hips bucked at the first flick of his tongue to her clit. She was swollen, ready to bloom in his mouth. He nuzzled in close to pull the throbbing bud into his mouth, sucking gently until she groaned and twisted his hair around her fingers. He worked the nub hard and fast with his mouth, alternating with an occasional nip to excite her to climax.

She came off the bed to hold his mouth close in her fever, crying out in her release.

Her shuddering aftermath slowed and he went to her, lying above her while she guided his cock to her pussy. He loved sex, loved the heat of it, the wild raw excitement of penetration, but with her it was an earthquake off the scales. He loved fucking her.

Gazing down at her expression of rapture, he knew everything he needed to know.

He had fallen in love with Carmen.

Chapter Eleven

Carmen devoured a third strip of bacon and bolted up-right in bed. "Ten o'clock! I'm supposed to be at Troost Elementary School in an hour."

Carrying her plate, Carmen got out of bed and ran into the kitchen. Don looked up from the frying pan where he stirred scrambled eggs.

"School?" He turned off the flame and wiped his hands on a dishtowel. "Some kind of drug bust?"

"Nothing so glamorous." She ran back into the bedroom to dress, searching under the bed for her shoes. "It's an officer friendly visit."

"You can't go like that. Half naked and looking sexy as hell." His grin was pure invitation, but she was on a mission. "What are you going to talk about?"

"How to stay away from men like you." She paused to kiss him on her way to the bathroom. "I have to get my car. You have to drive me to my apartment and then to the bar."

He followed, watching her from the doorway. "I'll get my stuff while you finish up."

She caught her reflection in the vanity mirror and warmed to the soles of her feet. She glowed with happiness. "Thanks, Don."

"I'm your man." He stepped into the bathroom to pat her ass. "Anything for my girl."

"I want you to go with me." She pretended to be absorbed in stacking her hair on top of her head, but her heart thundered while she waited for his answer. "I'm going in strapped."

He shook his head. "You want to drive those little boys wild?"

"No, I just want them to take me seriously." She turned to look at him, smiling with a bit of trepidation. "About going with me?"

"I'll stay in the shadows." He pulled gently on a wisp of a curl at her nape. "Of course I'll go. I wouldn't miss this."

Fifteen minutes later, they were in his car heading for her apartment. It was the first time they'd driven somewhere together that didn't involve hunting a drug dealer or chasing a murderer. Or, hurrying to have a round of fast sex.

His fast driving was something she'd always ragged him about, but today she overlooked it. There were more important things on her mind. He'd called her his girl. She faced the window and smiled, thinking about how easily he'd fallen into his current situation. Don may have been teasing, but she was serious. He didn't know it, but he'd always been her man.

She stopped him from getting out of the car when they parked in front of her apartment building. "Wait for me. I can change clothes easier without an audience."

He grinned and looked at his watch. "Okay babe, but shake a leg."

Carmen jumped and ran to the entrance, getting to her apartment in record time. It took several minutes, but she found her uniform in the back of the closet, still in a dry cleaning bag protector.

She ripped the cover off and laid the crisp blue uniform on the bed, then quickly shed her wrinkled shirt and blouse. She'd left her panties at Don's and pulled a fresh pair from the dresser along with a bra. Socks, she needed socks for the regulation shoes. She pulled on a pair and grimaced at the confinement of her feet.

Once she got the pants on, she pulled on the shirt, buttoned it and stuffed the hem into the waistband. From memory, she checked the brass with her fingertips, satisfied every button and emblem was accounted for. The patent dress Oxfords were still comfortable, and she laced them up in a hurry.

Okay, you're ready to face those kids. No you're not. They'll probably eat you for lunch.

She hadn't used the gun belt for a long time, and it weighed heavy on her hips. The Glock in the holster added another four pounds.

The sheet of rules from the school principal had disappeared, and she had no time to look for them. Don turned in the seat, watching as she flew out the door and ran to the car.

Applying lip-gloss after she climbed in, Carmen nodded. "Let's roll." He stared at her, smiling while he started the car. "What are you smiling at? Is everything straight?'

He shook his head, and whistled softly. "You're the best looking cop I've ever seen, Redstone. And hell yes, everything's straight. Lord."

Carmen re-checked the buttons of her shirt, making sure her uniform stood tall. She'd been so proud to wear it when she'd first gotten it, but just as eager to get back into street clothes to work vice.

She leaned back in the comfortable leather seat and exhaled, trying her best to not stare at him as they drove the short distance to The Shot. Being worried about her car had not occurred to her during the night. Who had time to think about a car while being entertained by Genonese?

The Lincoln was exactly where she'd parked it with all four wheels still attached. Don pulled up beside it and stopped. She looked at her watch and took a deep breath when she realized they had fifteen minutes to get to the school.

"I think we can make it using the side streets." She hopped out of his car and unlocked the driver's side door of her sedan. She pointed down the street. "Don't try to break ranks and go somewhere else." His expression of shock made her laugh.

"I'll be on your ass all the way, just like always." He revved the engine and grinned, waiting for her to take off.

Carmen chose Brookside Boulevard, the fastest, straightest route, glancing back occasionally to see Don following closely.

Worry about what she'd say to the kids began to nag at her confidence. Never having been around small children much, she began to panic.

They're going to hate you, Carmen. Suck it up and rely on Don to be your point man. He's probably good with kids.

* * * *

Don strode inside the limestone and red-brick schoolhouse behind Carmen, feasting on the feminine swish of her hips. She wouldn't look boyish if she'd been wearing a pair of coveralls.

He'd never seen her so animated as she smiled at Mrs. Grady, the tired-looking Principal walking them to the third graders' room. The place smelled like white paste, floor wax and books, a scent you never forgot.

Mrs. Grady opened the door to the room and gestured for him to join them. "In here, Captain Redstone."

Don wasn't worried about what would happen. Hell, he had twelve nieces and nephews and more on the way. Kids were little animals who made noise and left piles everywhere they went. They did what came naturally, and it didn't bother him.

Carmen turned to look at him, her lower lip caught in her teeth. He brushed his hand over her back, leaning close to reassure her. "You can take them, Carm."

He hadn't looked the class over until he stepped away from Carmen to give her the floor. Lord, what a bunch of future little bandits and speeders.

After Mrs. Grady's introduction, Carmen went into her spiel, looking like a cop should look. Clean and serious.

"I'm Captain Redstone with the Kansas City Police department." She smiled as the twenty-six kids yelled back their monotone greeting to her. "I won't bore you with a long list of reasons why I chose to become a police officer. I'd rather answer your questions."

Don laughed under his breath as the twenty-six pairs of eyes wandered around the room. The little brats were probably thinking of everything but conversation. Carmen moved out to the first row, looking at the kids with interest. She spoke to the biggest boy in the room, seated in a prominent position, probably to allow the teacher to keep an eye on him.

"You probably like football." Carmen held her hand out, shaking the kid's hand with no fear of the grime under his nails.

He grinned and nodded. "Yeah, me and my dad play when he comes over." He ducked his head and blushed.

Carmen glanced over her shoulder, seeking Don out, and he smiled his approval of her technique. She had a way with kids and didn't even know it.

Tentative in the beginning, she gained confidence, going from desk to desk to speak to the kids, one on one. Don leaned against the wall map to listen when she answered the questions the class asked.

"How'd a girl get to be a captain?" The football player tried to sound sarcastic with a swagger in his tone.

"I worked very hard, followed rules and thought about the rest of my squad." She pointed to her shield. "You earn these with honesty and caring about people."

Don had never heard Carmen talk about her job with such pride. He'd fallen for a beautiful, charming and loving woman. His personal admiration was interrupted by a tiny voice coming from a back row.

"Ma'am." A small, blonde girl shyly held up her hand, looking straight ahead as she spoke. "I want you to arrest Billy."

Carmen's attention riveted on the little girl with uncombed hair and huge blue eyes. "What's your name, honey?"

"Amy."

Don didn't miss the stiffening of Carmen's back as she moved between the desks to speak with the child. She'd sensed a problem in the girl's life. "Why do you want me to arrest Billy?"

"He hits me and pulls my hair."

A moment of concern hit Don in the gut. Carmen's cheeks pinked noticeably as she patted the girl's hand. "Is Billy here today?"

Mrs. Grady glanced at Don with a hint of worry in her eyes. She'd heard the stern authority in Carmen's voice, too. He tried to make eye contact with Carmen before she ripped into the kid.

Too late. The girl pointed to the redheaded, freckle-faced boy in the desk next to her. "That's him."

Instead of Carmen reaming the boy a new asshole like he'd expected her to do, she went to the front of the quiet room. She paced in front of the group several times before speaking to the class. "Sometimes, Amy, boys think hitting a girl shows their affection for that girl." Carmen clasped her hands behind her back, making her point without raising her voice. "What boys don't realize is how much stronger they are than girls. It doesn't show affection, it shows lack of consideration and it is wrong. Men do not hit women. Ever, Billy."

To his surprise, Billy, the hood in question nodded and apologized to Amy. Hell, it had to be love.

The half hour went quickly, and the kids crowded around to get the free tin badges the department had sent over for them. The boys wanted to look at Carmen's weapon and the girls all seemed intrigued with her hair.

Waiting for her turn, Amy shyly approached Carmen and hugged her around the waist.

Don's heart pounded with tenderness while Carmen embraced the little girl and stroked her hair. She straightened the belt holding up Amy's threadbare jeans and teased her into a laugh.

The woman scored a mega hit, with the kids all hugging her before filing out of the room and heading for the lunchroom.

When she had finished talking with Mrs. Grady, Carmen met his gaze and smiled, a flush on her cheeks.

He knew at that moment, nothing could change his feelings for Carmen.

Forever in love with Carmen, that's you Genonese.

Chapter Twelve

Carmen hated leaving Don after the wonderful morning they'd shared, but if she stayed with him, she'd never get to work on time.

She remembered to get her mail from the hall mailbox, waiting until she was inside her apartment before looking at the handful of bills and flyers. A folded piece of yellow paper caught her eye as it fell to the floor.

Reaching for it, she scowled at the grease spot on the paper. The kids down the hall must be putting things in mail boxes again. She tossed the scrap of paper onto the hall table and unbuckled her gun belt. Walking toward her bedroom, Carmen unbuttoned her uniform shirt and unzipped the trousers she no longer found so distasteful.

She had time to catch a nap and still get to the station on time. The sight of the half made bed didn't bother her. Don had slept there last night, and she happily lay down on his side, hugging his pillow, inhaling his scent.

Drifting off into a comfortable drowse, she paid little attention to the thumping against the outside wall. Her peaceful afternoon instantly ruptured by the sound of her car alarm blaring.

This was the second time in a week someone had set the thing off. She groaned and got up to hit the cancel button on her key pad. A look out the front window revealed exactly what she expected. Nothing.

Her yawn instantly stifled as she walked by the front door. Another yellow note had been shoved under the door. This time she picked it up.

She read the illegible written words several times. *You been warned bitch. Yur dead.*

Carmen had been called worse things and threatened, but never had the threat come into her home. She read the insane note again, torn between anger and worry. Who would dare come to her home, and how the hell did they know where she lived? If it had come from a previous arrest, which one?

She picked up the phone and hit Don's number, staring at the offensive scrap in her fingers.

When he answered his phone, he sounded sleepy. "Hi, sweet Carmen." He must have been resting well. His muffled groan made her wince with guilt. She knew firsthand how hard it was for cops to get enough sleep. "Can't get enough of me, huh?"

She exhaled, wishing she hadn't called him. "I may have a problem."

"I'll be right there." The sounds from his end of the connection told her he had gotten out of bed and was getting dressed. "Do you need a squad car?"

"No, I'm not sure it's even a problem. Yet."

After she hung up the phone, Carmen checked the doors and waited for Don. In her head, she ran a memory file of arrests she'd made in the last few months. They'd all made threats and screamed lawsuit. Nothing ever came of any of them. She finally decided she worried for nothing. Lots of kids around the area knew she was cop and probably thought it would be a cool joke to play on her.

She'd taken a shower and dressed in a white pants suit by the time Don arrived. He seemed anxious, scanning the apartment when she let him in.

"What's going on, Carm?"

"Maybe nothing." She loved being in his arms, being hugged close to his strong body. She may be a cop, but she was still a woman.

"Has to be something, or you wouldn't have called." He kissed her and gazed into her eyes.

"Just a series of silly stuff." She put all the little odd things into prospective and realized they weren't silly.

She picked up the greasy note and handed it to him, watching his normal, easy going expression freeze into anger. He took her hand and led her into the kitchen.

"We're treating this as a threat against you." He looked out the small window over the sink and closed the café curtains. "Get your purse and a couple changes of clothes."

"What?" She finally comprehended the meaning of his words. "Don. I'm not running from my home because of some coward's scribbling."

"Don't get stubborn on me, Carm." He rested his hands on her shoulders. "I don't mind sharing my sheets with you."

"Don't try to sweet talk me, Genonese." Her desire for independence wouldn't be taken down by this threat. "I love that you would share your home with me, but I'm a big girl."

"Redstone, you're a stubborn woman, but I think I know best this time." He jiggled her several times to get her attention. "I'll be worried about you and won't be able to do my job. You don't won't that on your conscience, do you?"

"I'm going to work, and so are you." She poured two cups of leftover breakfast coffee into mugs and set them in the microwave. "I'll do a search of the files and see if anything comes up. Okay?"

He shook his head and took the mug she handed him. "You know best, but don't think I will forget this."

"Oh, I know you won't." She dumped the coffee in the carafe into the sink. "Thank you for coming over. I'm okay now."

"Take this seriously, Carmen." He rinsed his cup and gazed steadily at her. "It has all the stink of someone wanting to get even."

Before he left, Carmen was aware of Don's looking at her window locks and deadbolt on her door. He wasn't stealthy enough to fool her. His concern warmed her heart, and she knew why she loved him.

Alone, Carmen went through the apartment to satisfy herself that the place had been locked tight. She left for work, knowing there would be little time for personal problems once she walked in the door.

With twenty minutes to fill before the new shift arrived, Carmen closed the door to her office and sat at her desk. She ran a checklist on her prior arrests made in the past year and took notes of the most sinister threats thrown at her. Filthy names didn't count.

None of them proved to be likely suspects, and most of them were serving sentences. She'd never worried about empty threats made in anger from the garbage. They were pissed because they'd been caught, nothing personal.

What a job, and you asked for it.

She sat up straight when her door opened and Gentry stepped into her office. "What can I do for you, Detective?"

He glanced at the screen of her computer. "Busy?" He sat in the chair in front of her desk. "Gotta say, Captain. You've cleaned this place up nice."

Carmen hadn't been fooled by his tea time conversation. He wanted something.

"Yeah, I'm a real homemaker." She closed out the screen on her computer. "What is it? A gripe from the ranks?"

"Not out loud." He laughed and straightened his flower-patterned tie. "I thought maybe you'd like company tonight on your rounds."

"Don put you up to this, didn't he?"

"Who?"

"You don't play stupid very well, Gentry." Carmen leaned across her desk to look him in the eye. "I don't need a babysitter." She looked up to see sergeant Rosen standing in the doorway. "Sergeant. I'll be out before the officers go on patrol."

"Well, that's not exactly what I wanted to see you about, Captain." He shifted from one foot to the other. "There's something you need to see in the men's public restroom."

"Okay." She didn't find it amusing as Gentry apparently did. She stood and followed Sergeant Rosen to the hall leading to the restrooms.

"I hate to ask you to come in here, but it's important." He went in first and opened the last stall door. "In here, ma'am."

Gentry followed close on her heels and leaned over her shoulder to read the magic marker graffiti. "Son-of-a-bitch." He scrubbed his hand over his mouth before apologizing. "Sorry, Captain."

She waved her hand to dismiss the apology. The crude drawing of a woman with a penis in her mouth didn't startle her. The name under it did. Captun Hore Redstone, blazed out at her in printed bold letters, underlined. An arrow pointed from the drawing's mouth to her name.

Inhaling a shaky breath, she crossed her arms over her chest. "That's plain enough."

"We'll get that cleaned off pronto." Sergeant Rosen was visibly angry, his dark eyes narrowed and words clipped as he added. "Sorry that happened."

"Don't you people watch who comes and goes in this place?" Gentry glared at sergeant Rosen.

"I just came on duty, Detective." Rosen glared back at the man who'd insulted his competence. "We can't lead all of the crazies by the hand."

Carmen ended the short confrontation. "No one's to blame. Sergeant Rosen is right, and I don't want this to go any further. Okay?"

"Well, we need to pick up all the freaks in the city and squeeze what we need out of them."

The sergeant rubbed his jaw and nodded. "It's somebody that knows your routine and where you work. Some degenerate that could hurt you, Captain."

She tried to laugh, but it sounded more like a sigh. "Stop worrying about this. I think it's a kid. An adult would have already come after me."

"Freaks like to taunt first." Gentry pointed to the offensive drawing. "It's somebody with zero IQ, which makes him even more dangerous."

"Let's go." She turned and headed off to let the evening patrol know she was around. She waited until the sergeant was out of earshot before cautioning Gentry. "Don't make too big a deal out of this, and don't make any special report to Genonese. He has enough to worry about."

"He's not going to take it worth a damn when he does find out."

"We're not going to tell him, are we?"

He didn't answer, simply straightened his tie before walking away to leave the building.

Carmen was surprised these men were so protective of her. She wasn't accustomed to being hovered over. The threats to kill her dredged up ugly memories from years ago.

That'll be the day, you son-of-a-bitch.

She shivered and hurried to the conference room.

Chapter Thirteen

Don heaved a sigh of relief, grateful to find a table at Anthony's this late in the evening. The corner restaurant had the best authentic Italian food in Kansas City next to his mom's cooking. He wished Carmen could have had dinner with him, but her shift had ended an hour earlier.

He frowned, puzzled that she hadn't called him before heading home.

Funny how he'd erased all other women from his life. Carmen effectively removed every memory of his pussy chasing days and enthroned herself as his woman. He got the feeling she didn't know how deep in his blood she had gotten. Getting close to her had been a hell of a job, and he still wasn't sure where he fit in her life.

He sipped the glass of Merlot he'd ordered, groaning softly when Gentry approached his corner table.

"Gentry." He gestured to the chair across from him. "What's up?" The detective seemed unusually quiet. He sat down and fiddled with the napkin wrapped silverware on the table. Don shook his head and moved the utensils out of Gentry's reach. "What's going on?"

"Redstone talk to you tonight?" Gentry helped himself to one of the breadsticks in the basket.

"I've been on duty and I assume so has she." The question had been innocent enough, but worry turned Don's nerves to liquid fire. "You want to talk, or do I choke it out of you?"

Gentry held his hands up. "No need for violence, my man." He glanced around. "It seems some prick has it in for her. Drew a nasty cartoon of her in the men's john sometime today."

Don tried to breathe against the squeeze of blood rushing through his heart. "What else?"

"The usual shit. You know, the old standby, I'm gonna get you, and you'll be sorry." Gentry gripped Don's wrist. "Settle down, boy. I'm taking a chance just telling you. She'll have my balls for this."

"I'm not going to kill anybody." Don couldn't hide his anger, adding finality to his comment. "Yet."

"Don't go off half cocked, son." Gentry pulled out his notebook. "You want to find out who's got an agenda, you talk to the wakadoos on the street."

"Yeah, I'll do that." Don took several bills from his wallet and threw them on the table before he stood up. "Dinner's on me."

Wisely, Gentry didn't follow him out of the restaurant. Don didn't want to be bothered. He planned to find the prick foolish enough to threaten his woman. More important, he wanted to be with Carmen to make damn sure no one gave her any trouble.

He got in his car and headed for her apartment. She'd had time to get home and he wanted to ask her about the wall art in the men's room. Doubt made him ease his foot off the gas pedal. The woman would resent his attempt to baby her and would be pissed off if he fired questions at her.

No babe in the woods, Carmen could smell trouble and take a man out before he had time to spit. Still, he had no plans to ignore his need to protect her. Maybe a quick cruise by her place, just to make sure. Hell, if he didn't ease his mind, he'd spend the night thinking the worse.

She lived not too far from the downtown district, one of those older places near the Plaza, but not yet called ritzy by land speculators. He didn't like the idea of her having a ground floor apartment. Too many windows with flimsy locks on them. Damn, he had to stop second guessing her decisions. She had never asked for his opinion.

He slowed the car and coasted past her building, trying to see lights in her windows. Too many shrubs to be sure if he saw her lights or the neighbors. He unclipped his cell phone and punched in her number.

Parking a few yards away from her building, he waited impatiently for her to answer. Relief flooded through his high-strung nerves when he heard her voice. Damn it! Her voice mail! He redialed and listened to her brisk recorded message again.

Still holding his phone in his fist, he thought over his options. Go to the door and surprise her, or go home and worry his ass off until he saw for himself she was okay.

He got out of his car and quietly closed the door.

After a look in the narrow walkway between the apartment buildings, he located Carmen's widows and looked into the dimly lit living room. The coffee table was clean, no keys and no phone. She wasn't home.

With his mind on Carmen's safety, Don walked toward the front of the building, his phone pressed to his ear. He stopped short. He didn't recognize the heavyset man trying the door handle. Not wanting to roust a guy if he lived in the building, he stayed in the shadows, giving the man time to go inside. After a couple minutes of observing the guy's attempts at the door, Don decided to move on him. When the man peered around the column of the small entry porch, the hair bristled on the back of Don's neck.

"Hey, buddy." Don moved quickly to stand in front of the stranger and block his escape. "I'm looking for a Jane Smith who lives on the first floor. Is she home?"

Suspicion radiated from the heavyset man's eyes as he answered in a swaggering attitude. "How the fuck would I know?"

"What do you know?" Don kept an eye on the man's hands. "Let's see some identification. Now!"

The glow from the overhead light bounced off the man's sweating forehead. He stepped to the side and tried a bluff. "Get out of my way, son-of-a-bitch, or I'll call the law."

"I am the law." Don motioned to the wall behind the man. "Kiss that stucco, and I mean now."

In an attempt to escape, the man tried to push Don aside, but found it impossible while caught in a headlock with his face scraping the wall. He screamed his indignation, kicking his legs out behind him.

"Think you're pretty tough, lawman?" Don heard spit hit the wall. "We'll, we ain't through with you."

"Rave on, prick." Don leaned on his prisoner, patting him down, remaining calm and resisting the urge to plant his foot in the asshole's crotch. "You carrying any needles, pipes, drugs or knives?"

"If I had any, you'd know it, pig."

"Is that a threat?" Don snapped his cuffs on the talkative prowler. "You have a name? I hate to keep calling you sweetheart."

The comment sent the man into an instant fight mode. His efforts to turn around only gained him another face scrubbing on the rough wall. "Lockard. Frank Lockard, you son-of-a-bitch."

Don reached into Lockard's right pants pocket, finding nothing but a little change and a snuff can. "That stuff will kill you." He patted the other pockets of the filthy cargo pants, hesitating before sliding his hand in a back pocket. He figured he'd found a needle, but it turned out to be a dull pencil.

He wondered what an animal like Lockard would be doing with a pencil. The answer came in a flutter of yellow that thudded to the concrete. Don picked up the note pad and lost his temper.

"What were you going to do with this?" He slapped the pad against the back of Lockard's head. "Writing your memoirs?"

"I want a lawyer. I got rights." Lockard continued to struggle against the cuffs and Don's weight pushing him into the wall. "I'm

Fast and Easy

not the only one doin' this. I ain't takin' the rap for a lousy hundred dollars."

"You're going to jail." Don turned his back to Lockard, leaning against him while he called for backup. His heart hammered crazily against his ribs. Carmen. He gripped the phone in his fingers, trying to stop their trembling.

His lungs would collapse if he didn't get hold of his rage. Not killing this piece of shit hurt like hell. He had to get rid of him and quick.

A squad car usually patrolled the neighborhood nearby, and Don was in no mood to pamper Lockard when the familiar dark blue sedan pulled up.

He dragged his prisoner to the patrol car, shoving him into the back seat after the officer opened the door. "I'll take him downtown.?" The officer slammed the door and approached Don. "What's he done, Genonese?"

"Threatening a police officer." Don ran for his car, yelling back over his shoulder. "I'll take care of the paper work. Don't worry about it."

Making a u-turn, Don headed for East patrol precinct.

He went against every instinct he had about calling her at the station and punched in the numbers to the sergeant's desk.

After what Don hoped sounded like a casual inquiry as to Captain. Redstone's whereabouts, Sergeant Rosen informed him she'd left an hour earlier, saying she planned to make a stop at headquarters downtown.

She might balk, but until this matter cleared up, she would have to put up with him twenty-four hours a day.

* * * *

Carmen wanted to go home and collapse into her bed, not spend time questioning a petty thief drug dealer. She worked her shoulders against a cramp in her neck, and waited for the officer to open the interrogation room door.

She instantly recognized the angry looking man sitting at the table. She remembered his straggly, thinning hair pulled back in a ridiculous ponytail and the teardrop tattooed at the corner of his right eye.

"Remember me?" She sat across from him, calculating the hate in his eyes. "I remember you. How's the knee?"

The officer that stood at the door stepped forward when the prisoner tried to stand up. "Sit."

"Yeah, I remember you." He pointed to the tattoo on his arm. "I got a name. Max Smith."

"Max Smith, I pulled your name out of the pot as the person responsible for the love notes I've been receiving."

Max grinned, revealing stained and broken teeth. "Now, why would I do that? Send the pig away, and I'll show you what I think of you."

Carmen longed to kick him out of his chair. It wouldn't help and she couldn't afford the trouble. "Assaulting an officer? Don't you have enough on your rap sheet?"

"I don't want to assault you. Just fuck you like a real man does." He put his cuffed hands on his crotch and shook his dick at her. "You like it in the ass? I'll even let you suck my cock."

"Very impressive, Max." She took the grease stained notes from her pocket and slid them across the table. "You're not smart enough to think this up on your own."

He nodded at the notes and snorted over a belly laugh. "I been in here waiting for my hearing. How am I gonna to do shit like that?" He shook his dick again, his whispered statement ominous. "Think a lot of yourself, don't you? You're not the only Redstone in town."

His meaning went through her brain like a shot.

"I'm the only one that can hurt you." Blood pumped furiously through her heart, and her lungs were squeezed under the pressure. "If the other Redstone is bothered in any way, don't count on leaving this place."

Max sneered and spat on the floor. "Ain't me, but you'd better hurry, cunt."

She glanced over her shoulder and held onto her temper. "Officer Ramirez." She maintained a cold outer appearance, but inside she boiled with fury. "You heard all this?"

"Most of it, ma'am."

"Good." She rose and walked to the door. "Take this snake back to his pit."

"When I get out, I'll let you eat my dick!" Max struggled against Officer Ramirez pulling him from the table. "Better yet, come by my cell and blow me."

She brushed off his last filthy words, too worried about her mother's safety. Running up the stairs instead of taking the elevator, Carmen gasped for breath. Fear made her deaf and blind to the sounds and sights around her and she reached the main floor before taking a deep breath.

The desk sergeant met her in the lobby, stopping her. "We have a silent alarm in the Quay district. Are you taking this call?"

She didn't wait to ask questions.

Momma.

On the way to her car, she checked the ammo in her weapon. There was no need to check. The Glock was never empty. This time, she planned to empty the semi-automatic into an animal's hide and hoped to hear him scream.

Her cell phone rang. She didn't want to, but she hit the answer button and yelled. "Redstone. What?"

"I know where you're going, Carmen. Stop right now and let the men in the district handle it."

"She's my mother, Genonese. I'm responsible for this." She gunned the sedan around a city bus. "I may be too late."

"Carmen!"

She threw the phone onto the seat and drove on, passing cars and swerving to miss a tamale wagon. Nothing would stop her, not even the devil himself.

Chapter Fourteen

Carmen reached her mother's house and pulled behind the patrol car already parked in front. The lights from the car seemed to set the area on fire. She could see the officers at the front door, using their cell phones.

She jumped out of her car and ran to the front door, holding her shield up for them to see. "What's going on? Why are you out here?" Controlling her fear and anger took all her effort.

"Ma'am, the suspect has a woman in there, and we've called for SWAT."

She unclipped her weapon, pushing past the surprised officers. "Come with me."

"Captain, he has the woman as a hostage." The patrolman's words only added fuel to the fire raging in her. She'd been in situations like this before, but now it involved a loved one. She wanted to throw all regulations aside and crush the animal who had dared harm her mother.

"And I said come with me." She pushed the door to the screened in porch open, moving quickly to the side door that led to the living room. "How do you know he has a hostage?"

To Carmen, it seemed to take an eternity to get information from the patrolman.

"He warned us not to come in, that he'd hurt the woman if we rushed him. He just wants out, he said."

At one end of the porch, an aging green leather glider moved slightly in the wind. A small wicker table had been overturned, and colorful beads glistened in brilliant disarray over a cream colored rug.

Carmen knew her mother sat out here in the evenings, creating new designs to please her loyal customers. Tonight, a beast had invaded her sanctuary and brought his stench with him.

She held her hand up to stop the two officers. "Did either of you see the woman? Goddamn it, is she okay?" She coughed and swallowed, trying to moisten her dry throat. "Is my mother in the same room with him?"

Rage consumed her as the officer nearest her grabbed her arm, trying to pull her away from the door. "Your mother!" He attempted to step in front of her, his voice husky with obvious strain. "Ma'am, you're not supposed to be here. You can't answer calls involving family members."

"Tell that shit to a cop whose mother isn't in there." She jerked her arm free. Hearing the wail of sirens, she clenched her teeth in frustration. If anything sent a nut completely over the edge, the sirens did. "Stand on either side of the door." She stepped on something soft and glanced down to see her mother's buckskin moccasin under her shoe. "I'm not playing with this bastard."

She didn't need the lights to find her way around the small home. The streetlight cast a warm glow over the thick, woven rugs and the floral arrangement on a rickety table. She released the safety on the Glock, gripping it in both hands as she moved forward.

Mere seconds clicked by, yet Carmen felt suspended in time, breathing from habit, locked in one bubble of space. The only sound coming from the small living room came in the soft chiming of the grandfather clock by the door.

Easing along the wall, she reached the open doorway to the living room. The scene flashing in silent clips before her took Carmen's breath. A man, wearing a white muscle shirt, held her mother in a headlock and peered out between the wooden slats of the blinds.

Carmen had been witness to this scene many times during her childhood. Everything around her evaporated, her heart beat drowning out any other sound. This could have been her drunken father throwing her mother around the room, kicking Carmen aside when she tried to intervene.

From her vantage point, Carmen could see the twist of pain on her mother's face. Desire to shatter the animal's skull that touched her mother became suffocating. He stood unaware of her presence, not realizing what an easy kill he had made of himself.. A tap on her shoulder reminded her she wasn't a murderer.

She motioned the patrolman to stand back. Familiar sounds of squad cars and boots on the concrete outside the house forced her hand, and she squared herself in the doorway.

"KCPD. Drop your weapon." She leveled her weapon at the stunned man's head. "Let her go."

Taken by surprise, he whirled to face Carmen, freezing where he stood after looking down the barrel of the Glock. Armed with a hunting knife, he made a cutting motion along his prisoner's throat.

"I'll slit her throat if you don't get out of my way."

Carmen's first thought hit like a cloudburst. *Shoot him.*

"You'll die." She moved another step inside the dimly lit room. "Momma. Are you hurt?"

"Carmen, leave now. Please." Her mother fought against the arm around her neck. The pleading in her voice fired Carmen's protective emotions to an all-consuming high.

She took another step, lowering her weapon while she spoke quietly to the man. "It's so easy to rough a woman up, isn't it?" She raised her Glock in reflex action, aiming for his head when he threw her mother off to the side where she crumpled on the floor. "That's not good enough, son-of-a-bitch." She reset the safety on her pistol, lowering it to her thigh. "Try me, he-man."

"Naw, I'd just have to kill you, bitch." He held the knife in his fist, holding in front of him and working it in tight arcs in a threatening motion. "Afore I slit you open, I'm gonna work on the old hag." He kicked the small woman on the floor in the back.

She didn't respond, but simply covered her head.

Carmen lost the thin line of control she'd been relying on.

She gripped the Glock in both hands, the safety released and her finger poised to pull the trigger.

"Carmen." Don's voice shattered the icy space behind her, splitting the deafening silence. "It's not worth it." He moved up behind her, reaching around to take her weapon.

"Back off, Genonese." She elbowed him for emphasis. "This doesn't concern you."

"You're an officer of the law, Redstone." He kept his weapon trained on the man wielding the knife. "He's scum. See the difference?"

Carmen heard the words and knew he told the truth, yet rage toward the beast near her mother wouldn't be so easily quelled. "I can't let him get off with a slap on the wrist."

She set the safety on her weapon and placed it on the bookcase by the door. The bravado had left the intruder's voice when he stared at the wall of police officers blocking his escape.

"Whatcha got on your mind, cunt?" He licked his lips and jabbed the knife in her direction.

"Kicking your ass, deviate." Carmen clenched her teeth, trying to pull her arm free of Don's restraining hand. "Come on prick, you and me. You like hurting women. Come on! Get your jollies."

Out of options and realizing he was finished, the trapped man gestured to Don who still had his weapon leveled on him. "Aw, hell, I ain't fightin' this bitch with half the fucking police department standing behind her." He tossed the knife aside and leered at her. "You ain't got nothing on me. I have rights."

Don's calming voice kept Carmen sane. "Put the bracelets on him, Redstone." He pulled his cuffs from his belt and pressed them into her hand. "Secure your prisoner, Captain."

She took dark pleasure from the fear in the man's eyes when she crossed the room and punched him in the shoulder. "Turn around, freak."

The steel bracelets were small payment for the abuse he'd inflicted here tonight, but his cry of pain when she squeezed the cuffs tight as possible sounded sweet to Carmen. She jerked his arms up until he yelped again before she shoved him toward the wall of blue uniforms.

"Momma, are you hurt bad?" Carmen knelt on the floor checking her for injury. "I'm taking you to the hospital."

To her amazement, she heard her mother laugh. "You are my angel girl." She stroked Carmen's cheek. "I'm fine, just a bruise here and there. He wasn't tough at all." Tears filled Carmen's eyes.

Sitting still for the quick check up by several EMT's must have taken a hell of a lot of restraint on her mother's part. Carmen stood close by, needing assurance her mother would be okay. She read impatience and a good amount of resentment on her mother's face during the examination.

After the crew left, Carmen breathed easier, letting the tension drift away. She hugged the woman that had given her life, thankful the episode hadn't dulled her humor. "Okay, if you won't go to the emergency room, you're coming home with me."

"This is my home, Carmen." Her mother held a hand up to Don after he gave custody of the intruder to the other officers to be escorted to a paddy wagon. He gently helped her to her feet. "What would happen if I left here? My friends would be worried, and my customers wouldn't know where to find me." She looked from Carmen to Don and nodded. "This is your bumble bee."

Flustered by her mother's reference to something private, Carmen hugged Ruby close, whispering in her ear. "He doesn't know that yet, momma."

"What's going on, ladies?" Don watched them with a perplexed smile. "Is something wrong?"

Carmen kissed Ruby's cheek and shook her head. "Nothing's wrong. She just wants to get her place straightened up." That had been weak, but she didn't want to include him in the family secrets yet.

He glanced around the sitting room, his all-seeing gaze settling on Ruby.

"If you want someone to stay here tonight, that can be arranged."

Ruby waved her hand, bending down to pick up an overturned table lamp. "That won't be necessary." She smiled at Carmen and patted her cheek. "I'll reset the alarm and lock the doors. I can take care of myself."

"Momma." Carmen huffed with concerned impatience. "I have paper work to do, and when I finish, I'll come back." At Ruby's look of parental disapproval, Carmen picked up her weapon and dropped it into her holster.

Already busy putting her home back in order, Ruby nodded. "If it will make you feel better." She paused as if taking silent inventory of Don's worth. "Come with me, Mister Bumble Bee. I make good coffee."

Carmen met Don's amused gaze and shrugged. "There's no reason we can't do our reports at the kitchen table."

They trailed after her tricky mother, Carmen jumping in surprise when Don's palm smacked her ass. She looked back to glare a silent warning to keep his hands to himself.

He caught her arm and pulled her back to lean against him. "Let's go talk about that bumble bee thing."

"You go out and get those report forms and forget what she said." Carmen wasn't secure enough about his feelings for her to discuss something so private. If only her mother would keep quiet. "Maybe we should go downtown and fill them out."

He inhaled roughly, and she sensed his irritation.

"I won't cause any trouble, babe." He touched her bottom lip with his thumb. "I'll get the forms from the patrolman outside. I'll leave as soon as we've finished them. Okay?"

He read her too well for comfort. What bothered her? His wanting to know more about her or the fact she knew very little about him?

"You don't have to run off." She heard her mother humming and the clink of the coffee pot being filled with water at the tap. "Momma does make great coffee."

"I'll be good." He gave her a quick kiss.

Carmen waited until he'd closed the screen door to caution her mother. "Momma, please don't discuss what we say in private."

Ruby arched her fine brows and shook her head. "I'm not wrong. He's a good man, rosebud."

"Don't say that in front of him. He'll think I've been talking sweet about him." Thinking hare-brained romantic crap about him was different than saying it. She didn't want to set herself up for his ridicule again. "Promise, Momma."

"I won't say a word." Ruby whispered. "He already knows how you feel about him."

* * * *

Don sipped his coffee and tried to concentrate on the paperwork in front of him. Damn near impossible while he observed Carmen and her mother interact. He'd never seen such love between a parent and child.

His gaze lingered on Carmen who seemed to have lost her fighting tiger personality as she easily laughed and joked with her mother.

Looking at the women with the same beautiful, sun-kissed skin tone and shining dark hair, he couldn't imagine anyone brutalizing them. Especially Carmen.

His gut clenched at the thought of her being abused and frightened. He now knew where she got her toughness and uncompromising character. He forced his attention back to the report, listening to the two women discuss jewelry and the flower garden out back. Their female chatter sounded great.

Carmen glanced his way, and of course he'd been eyeballing her. He emptied his cup and cleared his throat. "You finished, Carm?"

"About thirty minutes ago." Her beautiful lips parted in soft smile. She'd taken her hair down, letting it fall in a soft shimmer about her shoulders. "You need help with yours?"

"I finished twenty minutes ago."

She took his cup and rinsed it out at the sink. "It's two o'clock. You'd better get some sleep."

Her sexy smile tempted him to pull her into his arms and kiss her until she crawled all over him. He mentally shook himself back to reality.

Ruby took off her apron and hung it on a hook near the back door. She'd yawned several times, obviously hinting for him to leave. "Come back when you can, Don. Carmen will have to show you her baby pictures sometime."

He heard teasing in her voice and grinned at her. "It's a date, Ruby. Try to get some rest. Both of you."

Carmen grabbed her report and handed it to him. "Why don't you take these downtown right now? You seem to be no worse for wear."

He took the rolled up papers she poked at his chest. "Come outside with me, Carm."

"Why?"

"I have something to say."

She led the way to the front door and out onto the shadowed porch, turning to look at him as he caught her hand. "What do you want to say, Genonese?"

He knew the words by heart, yet saying them out loud, speaking of the racing excitement and passion in his soul stuck on the back of his tongue. He settled for something more immediate.

"I'll come by your place tomorrow." He pulled her close, trying to take a part of her scented warmth with him, to keep her close. "Is that okay?"

She slid her hands into his pants pockets, sending a line of fire through his body, and murmured her acceptance of his question.

"Only if you bring a change of clothes."

Chapter Fifteen

"Now you have to suck it." Carmen tightened her grip on Don's hair, smacking his cheek to emphasize her command. "Get busy, baby."

She loved his quick grin and the glint of desire in his dark eyes. And oh, his compliance to her lusty order. He lapped at the wine pooled in her belly button, moving down to suck on her clit until she squeezed her knees against his head. He'd brought her to climax completely and often in the last three hours, and always putting his needs aside while she'd exploded into a million joyous pieces.

Sprawled in the luxurious afterglow of amazing sex, Carmen sighed, watching him move up to lie beside her. His fingertips worked miracles, tracing small circles up her inner thigh to her throbbing pussy.

He squeezed her breast, gently nibbling the nipple. How long he could hold out with a hard on like he had now. His erection lay against her thigh, hot and heavy, revving up her need to have him completely.

"Fuck me, Genonese." Her breath caught in her throat as he braced himself over her, the tip of his cock pressing to her wet slit. "You do it so good."

The muscles of his back tensed, and she sensed he held back. To help him decide on now or later, she lifted her hips to take the first inch in, quickly wrapping her legs around his waist to pull him down.

He scored a deep hit, plunging to her the deepest part, groaning against her lips. "My God, Carmen. I think I'm going to come already."

His laugh had the texture of blue, cool smoke on a hot summer night. She clenched her pussy around his cock and lightly spanked his hard ass. "Give me what you've got fast and hard. I know you're good for another ride."

His kiss, like his slow push into her, went deep and tantalizing. She swallowed a scream as the overwhelming heat of passion threatened to lift her off the bed. He tasted her mouth, sucking her lower lip, inciting her to delicious madness as he drove into her with the power of a man hell bent on pleasuring a woman. A storm of awareness swept over her. He gave his all to her.

In a frenzy of orgasm too strong to hold down, Carmen tightened her legs around his hips and bucked to meet his thrusts, biting her lip to quiet the scream that defied her effort. It burst out, and she fell back in utter exhaustion as he came with a hard shudder and groan.

He calmed her heart rate by holding her in his arms, softly kissing her neck and shoulders until she could breathe normally. "Redstone, you're the best." He moved the bottle of wine off the bed to the nightstand. "I think…"

She's never known him to be at a loss for words. "You think what?" She rolled over to lie across his waist. "Tell me."

He played with a strand of her hair, obviously searching for words. "Rumor has it Gentry and Wells are engaged."

Not too happy to be discussing other people's nuptials, Carmen laughed dryly. "They deserve each other."

He didn't laugh or make further comment on the subject. He did pull her down to look into her eyes, his touch gentle as if he considered something she wouldn't like. Taming her, he'd called it once.

"We have one hour to check in at work." His mood changed back to teasing. "Maybe I'll call in sick. Woman, you have worn me thin."

Work. He'd made her forget where and who she had been before their sex marathon.

"Okay, get up and get the shower going." She didn't want to go to work, not with Don so close she could see the throb of a pulse in his temple. She looked out the window and sighed. "It's raining. That means wrecks and bums coming into the station for a place to dry out."

He got off the bed and picked up his clean clothes, and headed for the bathroom. "I'll get the water going, babe. Hurry and we can knock off another piece while we soap up each other."

His crude remark stung. Where had the sweet talking guy gone to? Carmen didn't understand her sudden desire to be wooed by the man she knew wasn't interested in her past a fast and easy fuck.

She bit back her disappointment and hurried to join him.

* * * *

Too tense too stay in her office, she got in her patrol car and cruised around the district, pleased with the lack of activity on the streets. A steady rain had slowed traffic to a decent level, and she relaxed.

She slowed at the intersection near a deserted park, blinking in surprise when a patrol car pulled in behind her, lights in the grill convincing her to pull over. Where had he been hiding? She unclipped her weapon. Anyone could put lights in their grill.

Whoever drove the car didn't get out right away. That made her nervous. She thought about the scum bags that had been hired to mess her up, and reached for her nightstick. She gripped it in her fist while keeping an eye on the car behind her. She didn't want to call for back up, but common sense won out and her hand went to her radio. She checked her rearview mirror one more time.

The guy getting out of the car didn't put on his hat or hesitate to stride toward her car. Her heart pounded with an adrenalin surge, and some fear. She flipped the switch of the searchlight on and directed it on him.

Genonese. She took a hard breath and dropped the nightstick. The beating of her heart now raced with excitement to see the man she loved. God, what a job.

She lowered her window and cooled her fight sensors by the time he tapped on the roof of her car.

"Okay, lady." Genonese trained his flashlight on her chest. "Out of the car."

She didn't care that it had started pouring rain. She opened the door and slid out, standing still while he looked her over. "What's the trouble, Officer?"

"Trouble is I'm crazy about you, Carmen Redstone."

Why had he chosen now to say that? What the hell had gotten into him?

"Oh, I get it. You're horny." She swiped rain from his forehead. "I can't have sex on the job."

"Carmen, listen to me." He gripped her shoulders, his words tripping over each other. "I want you for more than an occasional piece of ass."

She squinted in the lights glare, trying to read his expression. "Then, what do you want?"

"You. I want you for now and the rest of my life."

Soft thunder punctuated his words, covering her gulp. "I'm not going anywhere, Genonese. Are you okay?"

He pulled her into his arms, covering her mouth in a hard kiss before startling her with his sincerity. "I'll never be okay until I hear you say you love me." He squeezed her as if that would get the answer he wanted. "I love you, damn it. I loved you before you shot me in the ass, and it just gets stronger."

Carmen had waited a long time to hear him say the words, and she couldn't remember all the standard defense lines to cover hurt and disappointment. She didn't need them anymore.

"I love you, Don Genonese." It rained harder, and he held her tighter, the beat of his heart like a sweet touch of his hand. "Come by my apartment tonight. We'll see if you feel the same in a warm dry bed."

He hugged her hard, pulling her up on her tiptoes. "I'm spending every night at your place." Passing cars slowed to rubberneck at the scene taking place between them. "Duty calls, babe. I'll see you at home."

She got into her car and leaned out to kiss him one more time. "Just because I love you, don't think I won't use the cuffs."

"Use whatever turns you on, Carm." He stepped back when she started the car. "When do you want to get married?"

Married.

She jumped out of the car and ran after him. "I have to know one thing, Genonese." Damn it, why was she doing this? But she had to know. "Do think I'm fast and easy?"

"What a question." He tossed the flashlight into his car. "Damn it, woman. It took a hell of a long time to get you in bed. That wasn't fast or easy. Do you think I'm a prick?"

"I think you're the bumble bee I've waited for." She squeezed his hand, falling deeper in love with him with each drop of rain washing down her face.

"About that bumble bee thing." Don tried to grab her hand as she turned to leave.

"Family secret, Genonese. I'll tell you after we have a daughter."

THE END

www.bettywomack.net

SIREN PUBLISHING *Classic*

Taming Tessa

Betty Womack

TAMING TESSA

BETTY WOMACK
Copyright © 2011

Chapter One

Jack Savage had plans, none of which included driving from downtown Kansas City through the Plaza in rush hour traffic during a snowstorm.

An attorney should never be friends with a client. There were too many drawbacks, like playing chauffer to their brat sister, Teresa Duval.

Damn it. He had plans.

While he sat in the stalled traffic and waited for the snarl to unwind, he became more pissed off. Why would she need him to drive her anywhere? She had money and half a dozen cars.

Hell yes, he knew the answer. The chick just felt like having a servant that day. And he got the call.

Jack pulled up next to a Lamborghini in front of the address Duval gave him on the phone. Like every place on the Plaza, parking spaces were at a premium.

He glanced up at the windows of the building, groaning at the thought of going inside. The Walnuts on the Plaza was the hottest address in Kansas City to live for people with money to burn.

He'd probably get a ticket for double parking. Drake Duval could pay this one. Jack pulled the keys from the ignition of his sedan and got out. He trudged through the snow and ran up the steps to the front entrance of the building.

The doorman scowled at him long and hard before opening the heavy glass door.

"Ms. Duval is expecting me." Jack brushed snow from the shoulders of his black wool overcoat.

"Shall I announce you, sir?"

What the hell did he look like to the snooty bastard? Some kind of derelict? "No need. She probably knows her ride is here, been looking out the window at all the sliding cars in the pretty snow." The doorman's eyes rounded at Jack's flip reply. "I'll just be going on up and getting Ms. Duval if you'll tell me the apartment number."

Jack was positive that the stone-faced little man sniffed with indignation.

"Mr. Link Griffin owns the apartment. I'm not sure he'd approve of Ms. Duval inviting company in."

What made people want to be such hard asses? Especially today when he had a couple dozen things to accomplish in the next two hours.

"The number, please."

"Six sixty-nine. The only unit on the floor."

That fucking figured. Griffin needed lots of room for his women and trust fund money. "Thanks, friend. Maybe we can have a beer after work tonight."

"I hardly think we would have anything in common, sir."

Jack laughed at the man's answer. He probably thought he'd lift his wallet.

He got off the slowest elevator in history to find himself in a fancy outer hallway on the sixth floor. The ritzy apartments were off limits unless you were invited in. The place smelled of money—lots of it.

Okay, now see if the little lady is ready for her taxi.

His moment of levity vanished when he saw the door to six sixty-nine slightly ajar. Son of a bitch. Blood.

The blood spatters began at the door and continued on to the service exit door at the end of the curving hallway. The door to the stairway yawned wide open.

A stab of cold worry hit his gut.

Tessa!

He rapped hard on the door, waiting for someone to say something.

Shit.

He looked down at the drying blood on the sand-colored carpet. Hell with waiting any longer. He shouldered the door open and went inside the quiet entry hall.

Big and void of any sign of life. A sea horse fountain splashed uselessly in the center of the entry hall. Another damned receiving area. All that empty space sure made a guy feel welcome.

"Tessa." He didn't like the eerie silence. Anywhere Tessa happened to be, noise followed. Right now he'd give anything to hear that cultured voice.

The double doors to the formal living room stood wide open. That didn't mean a thing. The woman probably never closed a door or drawer after herself.

"Tessa!"

He wasn't ticked now. His hair prickled at the back of his neck. A pile of white towels on the floor were stained a dark plum color, releasing the scent of fresh blood as warm air circulated in the room.

Band-aids and small, bloody gauze were scattered around the fancy décor. Cotton swabs had been tossed in an ashtray. Someone had something bleeding.

"Tessa!"

No time to be cautious. He rushed from room to room, opening closets and looking under beds. He would have bypassed it, but the drapes on the terrace doors fluttered slightly.

Jack picked up a heavy brass figurine of a naked chick and slowly pulled the drapes apart. He wasn't quite six feet, weighing one eighty, and dreaded a fight with Griffin's goons.

He clenched his teeth, prepared to defend Tessa from whoever hurt her.

The doors were open only a crack, but cold air poured in the room. He shoved the doors open wide and stepped outside, squinting against the wind-driven sleet.

He flinched when he saw crimson stains on the skiff of snow covering the brick terrace floor, but that wasn't what held Jack's attention.

Teresa Duval pressed her body to the icy wall, staring at him with suspicion-filled eyes.

"Tessa." He spoke softly, moving toward her. "Come inside."

For one agonizing second, she appeared ready to run for the rail. Instead, she lifted her hand and pointed to the terrace door, still hugging the damn wall.

She whispered, obviously afraid of being overheard. "Is he dead?"

"Should he be?"

"I tried to kill him."

Jack relaxed a little, figuring there hadn't been a murder committed yet. "You caused all this mess? What in the hell did you hit him with?"

"My fist." She looked ready to cry, and her chin quivered while she spoke. "I told him he was getting drunk and he slapped me. I hit him in the mouth because it hurt." She trembled, obviously frightened. "I ran and he chased me, screaming that I was a cheap whore. He caught me and started beating me. That's when I hit him in the nose."

Jack couldn't help it. The low chuckle wouldn't stay quiet. That explained all the blood.

"Tessa, I'm calling the cops just to be on the safe side. Griffin may press charges against you." The roll of her eyes triggered his disgust again. "It always helps if the assailant feels compassion for her victim."

She bit her lip and grimaced. "I don't feel compassion."

"I know that, but you can pretend for once, can't you?" He held the phone up to drive his point home. "To keep your ass out of a cell downtown?"

She went pale with fright at the thought, looking ready to bolt again, while he punched in the numbers to the downtown precinct. The operator connected him to Detective Dave Dresslehouse's desk.

"Yeah, hey, Dresslehouse, Savage here." Jack glanced at Tessa, making sure she stayed put. "I'm removing a young woman from an apartment where an altercation took place."

Jack could hear his friend laughing. "You involved in it, Savage?"

"No. Just taking the lady home. There were a few punches thrown and some blood drawn. Nobody for the morgue, but the bastard that got hit is bleeding. From what I hear, he probably has a broken nose." He moved away from Tessa while he finished his call. "She stood up for herself. There was no attack. Just self defense."

He lowered his voice and finished his conversation. "Her family wouldn't want this to get out. I'd appreciate it if you contacted me if there is a follow up investigation."

After giving the detective all the details he could furnish, Jack closed his phone and looked at Tessa.

He wanted to shake her when signs of regret set in. She looked contrite and beautiful.

"Are you sure I didn't kill him?"

"Griffin isn't dead. No bleeding corpses have been turned in." Her look of fear made him soften his tone. "The detective said he'd check it out for me. He said the bastard is probably being patched up at Research Hospital right now and will be out carousing around by tomorrow night."

Jack couldn't work up any sympathy for the son of a bitch in question. Hearing the news that her latest boyfriend had survived didn't seem to reassure the beauty hugging the wall.

What an opening for him to ask why the hell she put up with the woman-beating party boy. Jack wouldn't say what he thought out loud. He had to get her out of the apartment fast.

His gaze fell to the stains on her coat. "None of this blood came from you, did it?"

She shook her head and barely glanced at her ruined ermine. "I have to go see how he is, or he'll…"

"Or he'll beat the hell out of you?"

Keep your mouth shut, Savage. What she does is none of your business, God damn it.

Something changed in her attitude after his personal dig.

Her long, pale-blonde hair lifted in a blustering gust of wind and moved about her chapped face. With the grace of a pampered chick, she pulled her ermine coat closer about her slender body and lifted her chin.

Such a beautiful woman and so damn messed up. Why the hell did he care? He'd gotten tired of stepping around the truth about her lifestyle, ignoring her split lips and bruised cheeks. He wanted to pull her close and tell her how deep his feelings ran for her. He was in love with her and didn't know exactly when it happened. Maybe the first time she really looked at him. His life had changed in that moment and Tessa owned him, lock, stock, and bleeding heart.

Tessa spoke at last. "That's none of your business, Savage."

What did it matter to him if she left with him or not? He knew one thing for sure. Her bullshit made him tired and really cranky.

"Tessa." He stepped toward her. "I don't give a rat's ass what's going on in your crazy life. Your brother's the one concerned about you. Not me."

She gave him a dubious once over. "Then why are you here?"

"I'm being paid."

"You're a flunky."

"That's a compliment coming from a trick like you."

Aw, hell. Why had he said that? Trading verbal punches with a chick wasn't his style. He had to question his own sanity, standing out in the bitter December weather with an aggravating broad. He had to catch a flight home to Sedona, not stand around, freezing his ass off in Kansas City.

Sudden movement from her area of the terrace indicated she'd gotten cold enough to seek shelter. Her shoulders moved in a shudder as she spoke.

"I want to go home."

Jack pointed to the open doors. "Your servant, ma'am."

If he read the message in her glower correctly, she considered him scum beneath her feet and he'd better step aside while her majesty made an exit from the frigid cold terrace.

She went back into the lavish apartment and grabbed her small handbag from the floor. Walking behind her, Jack checked her out like he always did. She had the sweetest ass he'd ever seen.

They took the slow elevator down to the lobby and escaped the doorman's notice. Jack thought he might have rushed Tessa a little too hard when she lost her shoes.

He groaned, gathering them up and kneeling down for her to stick her small feet back into the ridiculous slides.

"Great winter shoes there, lady."

Outside in the crackling cold air, her tawny eyes lingered on him longer than usual.

Oh no, man. Don't get carried away by one look of pity from this one. Not unless she begs you.

"Savage."

He stopped mentally taking off her clothes.

"Yeah, Tessa."

He expected trouble when she looked up at Griffin's windows.

"I can call a taxi." She covered the lower half of her face with the collar of her plush coat. "I know you hate being around me. Drake shouldn't have bothered you."

Jack weighed the honesty of her words against her true personality. She loved screwing with his mind.

"No trouble, Tessa." He took her arm and led her to his car. The windshield had disappeared under a blanket of snow. He opened the door for her, hoping she found the sedan worthy of her supreme highness. "Get in."

She didn't have to say anything. Her cat eyes spoke clearly. She resented doing anything he suggested. Damn, what a gorgeous woman. Too bad all that silky skin covered a scheming, hell-bent-for-trouble witch. He couldn't be too pissed after noticing the spray of blood on her sleeve.

Griffin had better walk easy from now on.

They rode in silence for several blocks, the episode in the apartment sticking in Jack's mind. He hated dead silence, and hell yes, he felt protective toward her.

He had to say something to her. She paled and glanced at him from the corner of her eyes. Man, she couldn't be scared of him, could she?

"Are you worried? About what Griffin will do?"

She shook her head and stared out the window, making small circles on the fogged up glass. After what seemed like hours to him, she hit him with a bombshell.

"Will you take me home with you?"

She sat placid as a cherub now, sweet and soft looking, while TNT exploded under his ass. "What?"

He thought he'd misunderstood her.

Her frown said she saw him as a little slow. "Home. With you." Her dainty shoulders lifted while she waited for his numb tongue to flap. "Well?"

Chapter Two

Could she be so repulsive to him? His shell-shocked expression had been proof enough that he'd rather drive off a bridge. She didn't ask again until he stopped the car in front of her townhouse.

"So, Savage?"

"So, Tessa?"

Damn him. He'd forced her to beg. She didn't like him that much. "Okay, I'll say it again just to see that scared rabbit look on your face." She turned to meet his steady gaze. "Me, staying at your place for a few days."

He stared at her as if she'd turned green and grown a horn on her forehead.

"Did it ever occur to you, lady, that I might have something to do?" He flicked his hand toward her in open impatience. "You'll be fine. If you're scared of Griffin, tell security to keep him off the premises."

"He said he would kill me." As luck would have it, her voice broke on the last word. Maybe he would feel sorry for her.

He remained resolute, leaning over to open the door for her. "Stay with Drake. Its two days until Christmas. He's your brother, for Christ's sake."

His suggestion would have been good for anyone but Tessa. Constant war raged between her and her brother. He'd controlled her life and her money until her twenty-second birthday. Until that time, she relied on him for everything, and he routinely invaded her privacy. Now, she had no idea how many millions she had and enjoyed spending it on everything and anything she wanted. That included men she liked.

Funny how she'd never noticed Jack's dark eyes. "Drake is out of town by now. I'll be alone. And scared."

"Do me a favor, Tessa." His sensuous cologne snaked around her in a warm lei of exotic fragrance. "Get out. I have a plane to catch."

Her heart pounded with the hurt of his rejection and growing anger. "You jerk. You can't believe I meant any of that." She would have tumbled from the car if he hadn't caught her wrist. "You're the last man I would spend Christmas with."

Her exit would not be the theatrical scene she'd hoped to pull off. She stumbled and slid, legs straddled and skirt hiked to her ass. The ultimate disgrace came as she fell out of her shoes for the second time that day. No, now came the most unforgivable act, falling onto her back in the snow.

She heard the car door slam, but managed to scramble to her feet before Jack could get to her.

"Let me help you." He had the balls to laugh at her. "You trying out for the hockey team?"

"Get away." She slapped his hand aside. "I don't need your help. Go catch your plane to hell.'

He stood back while she scrounged around for her shoes. "Need help yet, Cinderella?"

She couldn't think of anything dirty enough to call him. Carrying a shoe in each hand, she brushed past him, stomping up the walkway to her front door.

Her bare feet burned from the cold and her lips were numb. She hated herself for letting him see her in such a ridiculous situation.

At the door, she hesitated and glanced at him over her shoulder. Mister Cool watched her every move. Getting the key in the lock seemed to take forever. She finally heard the lock click and pushed the door open.

Once safely inside with the door closed, she looked out the peephole to see him driving away. The weight of being alone settled on her shoulders.

She called herself an idiot, watching the red tail lights of Jack's car disappear in the swirling snow.

Why weren't you nicer to him? He would have stayed if you'd treated him right. If you could have made him forget how much he dislikes you.

Maybe she should call the hospital and ask Griffin if he wanted to make up.

Her soft groan was the only sound in the dimly lit hallway.

Don't be a fool, Tessa. That relationship ended when you broke his pretty nose.

She knew that didn't matter. There had never been anything between them. They used each other as party dates because neither of them had anyone to care about.

Spending the night alone made her nervous. If it hadn't been storming, she'd go to one of the trendy clubs on the Plaza, maybe meet someone new.

She sighed and made a halfhearted attempt to hang up her coat. The expensive garment fell unnoticed to the floor. Out of habit, she went through the house, flipping on lights. The fact shamed her, but she feared what she couldn't see in the dark.

A thumping sound from the upper level startled her. What if someone had gotten in and hid upstairs? That was stupid thinking. The door had been locked when she came home. No one else had a key.

Okay, so you don't have to go up there right now.

The kitchen seemed the best place to wait for her courage to return. Tessa dropped her handbag on the hall table and walked into the gleaming chrome and granite kitchen. Her grandmother's service of Bavarian china and Waterford crystal sparkled in the dish cabinets. She had never used it.

Her gaze went to the stack of unopened mail on the counter where she'd dropped it several days ago. She sorted through the envelopes, tossing most of it aside. The postcard with a pretty winter scene held her attention. The note had come from her brother Drake. He'd sent a last minute invitation for her to join the family at their Squaw Creek lodge in Colorado. Sure, and be bored, questioned, and badgered by her family.

She glanced around the kitchen and made the decision of a lifetime. In the morning, she would call Drake. Better to be with her tight-assed brother than alone.

Feeling hopeful and somewhat eager, Tessa hurried up the stairs to her bedroom to pack. She laid out enough clothing for a week. That meant several suitcases for all the shoes, boots, and cosmetics that would be needed.

Thirty minutes later, she became tired of packing. Why hadn't she hired that live-in maid to do all this? She knew she'd turned that down because Drake had suggested it.

Tessa didn't want someone else in the house. It would have ended what little privacy she enjoyed. She valued that too much to give it up.

On the flip side, she wondered how living with Jack would be. He was too good looking not to be involved with someone special. Her chances with him had been zero from the day they'd met. Being her brother's attorney and friend, the chances were zero to nothing.

She remembered their first meeting. He'd walked in just in time to witness a screaming brawl between her and Drake. She couldn't remember the reason for the fight, but she did remember Jack's expression. He'd been amused.

Plus, he probably thought she was a trollop, easy and available to any shithead that came along. Maybe because he'd seen her with a lot of different men.

To hell with him.

She threw a catalog on the floor in disgust.

He didn't know her at all, and it looked like he didn't want that to change.

The small snapshot of Drake on her desk caught her eye. She wondered what he had in common with Savage. For that matter, how old was Jack Savage? He was in his late thirties, early forties maybe. No gray hair and his teeth were white when he laughed. Even if it happened to be at her.

She loved his laugh and warmed to her bones whenever he smiled at her. From their first meeting, he'd moved into her heart and there had been no room for anyone else.

* * * *

Jack leaned against the window casing and stared morosely down at the snow piling up on the side street where he lived on the re-emerging West Side. He'd moved into this neighborhood for the quiet and the fantastic view of the river and old rail yard.

There was something comforting about living near the abandoned stockyards. The West was never far away.

People like Tessa and Drake Duval were messing with his peace and quiet, and he didn't like it.

Drake had a huge set of balls to ask this of him. Being with Tessa compared to a hot summer whirlwind with a crazy witch in the center. A sexy, mouthy witch.

He figured he'd be lucky to get to the airport at all. He sipped his cognac, the last in the house, and thought about what he'd done earlier that evening.

Not much of a hero, you bastard.

Tessa hadn't been out of his thoughts since he'd left her. He was being ridiculous. The woman was just that—a woman, and a damn tough one at that. Why was he worried about her? If he didn't stop thinking that way, she'd ruin the holidays with his family and friends.

Think about the parties and women you're going to miss. Mom's fabulous meals. The women. Aw, shit!

Jack was furious with himself, but grabbed his overcoat and keys, slamming the door as he left to go pick up the world's biggest nuisance: Tessa.

He had been kidding himself, knowing from the start he was going back for her. He hated like hell to call his parents with the lame excuse that he was busy and wouldn't be home for Christmas.

He heard the disappointment in his mother's voice now and her saying she understood. He sure as hell didn't.

Driving the hazardous streets to pick up a woman he had no desire to spend time with gave him reason to question his mental capacity.

He clenched his teeth as a skidding city bus groaned past him and hit a traffic light. Not only was he crazy, he was a danger to himself. Hell fire. He was from Arizona. What the hell did he know about snow and ice? Nothing.

That settled it. If he did manage to get Tessa and himself back to his place, they weren't leaving till spring thaw. He wondered just how safe they would be from each other, caged up in his bachelor pad.

After witnessing a dozen collisions on the way to her place, he breathed easier. He pulled up in front of Tessa's townhouse, grinning when he noticed all the lights were on.

He got out of the car and glanced around the area, a habit all attorneys were wise to adopt. He never knew when an unhappy felon wanted his head.

There was at least another three inches of fresh powder on the walk. He plowed through it while his dress shoes filled with snow. Why the hell hadn't he changed his clothes? His earlier thought that he might like the fresh, crisp scent of the air died a quick death. There wasn't anything good about this weather.

He tried the bell and then pounded on the door. There was no response.

"Tessa." He stomped his feet, testing to make sure they weren't frozen. "Open the door, damn it."

The doorknob turned, but nothing else happened. He grimaced, wondering what was going on. Laying his shoulder against the sturdy door, he pushed with all his strength.

He couldn't believe it. He was airborne.

Whoa, damn it!

That's all he had time to think while he flailed his arms and spreads his legs on the slick tile floor, then fell face down in Tessa's hallway. When he slid to a stop and looked up, she stood over him, her smile taunting.

"Hello, Jack."

"Why don't you lock your damn door?" There was no dignity or anything close for him to grab on to. "Get your stuff. You're going home with me."

"What made you change your mind?" Her smile was smug, and her eyes sparkled with what she probably considered a victory.

"You looked like you could use a vacation." His back hurt when he got up to stand face to face with her.

He calculated their lips would have no trouble locking since she was almost as tall as him. His fingers itched to cup her pretty chin and trace the fine line of her jaw. He was getting hard just being this close to her. Would her breasts fit in his hands?

"Jack?" She moved a fraction of an inch closer to him, smothering him with her sensuality. "I'll go get my things."

He woke from his erotic fog with a start. "Hurry it up. The car will be ice cold if you keep screwing around."

Such a witty choice of words. Her soft laughter clung to him long after she'd walked serenely up the stairs, leaving him to think about the way her hips looked as she walked.

While she was upstairs humming, he paced the floor and called himself a fool.

What was he going to do with a woman so rich her fur coat lay in a heap on the floor? He picked it up and hung it on a fancy oak hall tree.

He looked around, taking in the fine brocade couches and designer club chairs in front of the stone fireplace. There had never been a fire in that thing.

The liquor cabinet was a glass affair filled with bottles of fancy labels he'd never considered buying. He was surprised to see she hadn't opened any of them.

He wondered what she would think of his two bottles, one scotch and a half bottle of cognac. Hell, he didn't care what she thought. He was going to treat her just like he always did.

You're kidding yourself, Savage. This is going to be different, and you're worried about being alone with her.

He hoped he could keep his desire for her his secret problem.

"It's about time." His gruff comment spewed from his open mouth when Tessa came down the stairs. She looked sensational in a black coat that hit the floor and fit her waist like a hug. Her long blonde hair hid under a red tam on her head.

"I hope I wasn't too long." Her gaze darted from him to the two suitcases she'd pushed down the stairs. "Is this too much?"

"Is it enough to last until March?" Her eyes rounded with shock. "Relax. We'll kill each other before then."

She reached for one of the bags. "I'll be gone long before I have to put you out of your misery."

"You got that right, sister." Jack grabbed both bags. "Open the door and lock it after we're out."

"Let me have one." Her offer sounded limp as he hurried out the door, fighting two heavy bags to the car.

"Get in the car…please." Jack threw the bags in the trunk and stomped his way back to the front of the car. He got in and turned the heater to full blast.

She huddled in her coat, watching him with a wariness he hated. He decided to ignore her and try to get home with as little trouble as possible.

What happened once they were alone in his apartment was not going to be pretty. Why had he chosen to stay here in the frozen wastes of the Midwest? Tessa had nothing to do with his decision.

Liar.

Chapter Three

"You're mad." Of course he was mad. He probably had planned to be with someone he cared for.

"That's not even close." His dark gaze drilled into her long enough to say how despicable he found her.

She knew one way of changing his mind. She would have sex with Jack. Maybe.

He didn't speak again until they got to his apartment. "We're here, ma'am."

She made a face of distaste. He lived in a two-story salt-box brick house. It sat perched on the edge of a cliff and overlooked nothing but a rusting rail yard and abandoned warehouses.

He got her bags from the trunk. "You can look out a window where it's warm." She knew he was strong when he easily lifted both bags and ran up the short flight of steps. He unlocked the door and set her bags inside. "Well, come on in. It's reasonably clean."

She didn't doubt that. He was always neat and smelled so damn good. "Where am I to sleep?"

"With me." A hint of a teasing smile played over his sensuous mouth. "You got a problem with that?"

"Not at all." He probably thought she was teasing. She wasn't.

"Don't get excited, Tessa. I have two bedrooms."

He broke her bubble easily enough.

The inside of his house smelled like him—clean and exotically male. She took off her coat and draped it over a cocoa-brown armchair.

"They've invented a place in the wall for that." He took the coat and handed it back to her. "I'll show you where your closet is."

"My things?" He was already halfway up the winding staircase, carrying her bags.

"Later." He eyed her with a slight smile. "Right now, I want to get you settled in your bedroom."

What was that little smile—a tease, a warning, or indigestion?

"I'm ready if you are." She followed him to the upper level, hating to admit that the place was nicely furnished and spotless.

"This is where you'll bunk." He flipped the light switch and the room came alive with warmth. "Plenty of room for you and all your stuff." He nodded to an open door across the room. "Your private bath."

"Do you have candles?" He arched his dark brows. "I always have candles in my bathroom."

"What do you take me for?" He tossed her coat onto the white down comforter on the bed. "You'll make it without them. Or do you need me to scrub your back?"

"If you're offering, it would be a nice change from your hostile self."

"Oh, this is going to be fun." His mumbled words made her smile.

"What did you say, Jack?"

"I said yes, ma'am."

He went back downstairs, leaving her to explore.

He liked comfort and no clutter. The bed was a nice big one, covered with a sea-blue down comforter and a folded green blanket at the foot. He also liked to be warm.

Thinking there might be leftover women's things in the double closet, she opened the doors. The soft familiar scent of his cologne was the only occupant.

That was going to change right now. She hurried to open her luggage and began to hang up her clothes.

"Tessa." She swung around, surprised to see him in the doorway.

"What's wrong?" Maybe he was going to take her back home. She closed the closet doors. "Has Griffin found me?"

"Wouldn't matter if he did." Jack handed her towels and washcloths. "I can handle that."

Her stomach churned, and she hugged the towels to her chest. "He's cruel."

"And I have a thirty-eight."

"Really?" Jack fascinated her even more now, and his cool demeanor fired her attraction to him. The idea he would protect her made her love him more.

He paused at the door, turning to look at her. "I really wanted to tell you there are no strings attached to this. Okay?"

Okay, that proves he isn't attracted to you.

She turned down the comforter. "I didn't think so."

He drummed his fingers on the door and smiled at her. "I'll try to find something for you to eat."

She'd always wondered how being alone with him would be. None of her ideas had been accurate. The idea that he felt nothing for her hit like a ton of bricks.

She remembered the way he'd gone out of his way to avoid her, leaving Drake's office the moment she showed up. Much to her shame, she'd driven by Drake's office on a regular basis just to see if Jack was there.

He'd made it crystal clear she wasn't the girl of his dreams. But maybe she'd be the woman he couldn't forget.

The aroma of coffee made her lick her lips. Something else smelled wonderful, and she realized she hadn't eaten since lunch yesterday.

He'd changed while she had been snooping. She'd never seen him in faded jeans and a dark blue flannel shirt. They looked good on him.

"That smells good." Tessa looked at the table he'd set for two. "What is it?"

"Porterhouse steak and scalloped potatoes." He frowned at her questioning of the fare. "It's tomato soup and butter sandwiches."

"Just like on television. Perfect." She'd never had a butter sandwich, but they looked heavenly.

"Just eat it and keep your compliments to yourself."

She hadn't meant to piss him off, but she always seemed to rub him the wrong way. "Okay."

He sat down and began to eat, glancing at her from time to time. "What?"

"I like it." That wasn't a lie, and she smiled, chewing the slightly dry bread. "I'll clean up after we eat."

"I have a dishwasher." He poured two cups of coffee from the carafe he'd set on the table, sipping his, and shoving the creamer across the table. "I hope you don't take sugar."

She didn't ask why. He was a man alone and probably didn't eat at home often.

"No, this is great like it is." Tessa ate quickly, finishing her soup like a starving kid. "May I have a refill?"

She held her bowl out to him.

"Got plenty and you can help yourself."

While she refilled her bowl, she tried to make conversation. "What do you do with your spare time, Jack?"

He got up and set his bowl in the sink. "You don't have to make small talk." His dark gaze made a quick survey of her before he spoke again. "Finish your meal. I'm going to see what the forecast is."

Just how hot did he find her?

His coolness was wearing thin and he'd find out between now and morning she wasn't to be ignored. He'd go down in flames.

Finishing the soup wasn't hard. It was delicious. After polishing off a second sandwich, she sought out the man she'd soon call her own.

She found him in the living room, deeply absorbed in something on his laptop.

He looked so comfortable, she wanted to mess with his bear trap mind. She barely earned a glance from him upon her entrance.

"What are you doing?" She smirked, hoping to get a response from him. "Writing to Mommy?"

"Since there's nothing going on here, I'm finishing up some things I should have gotten to earlier." He grimaced, apparently losing his concentration. "It's called work."

He was insulting her, not subtly, but mean and angrily.

"There's nothing going on here because you're a jerk." Tessa wanted to throw a chair at him for all his hateful comments. "Let's get this clear between us. I wouldn't fuck a man like you. You probably don't know how to do anything but grunt."

Her tirade ended and he stared at her with a grin. "Well damn, Tessa." He closed the laptop. "Is that what you're accustomed to?"

"This isn't about me." She glared at him. "You seem to think I want in your pants. That's a laugh. I don't like horseshit on my sheets."

"I'll keep that in mind." He turned the sound up on the TV. "I told you no strings and I meant it."

She couldn't stop. Tessa hated the condescending tone of his voice. She'd heard it all her life.

"Thank you so much, Jack." She glanced out triple windows that overlooked a small yard. It was dark and she was stung by the loneliness creeping around her. "See to it you stay in your own room and don't accidently wander into mine."

She stomped off to take the stairs two at a time, afraid he'd have a nasty comeback for her warning.

God, she hadn't meant any of it. She couldn't stop the tug of war being waged inside her. The more he resisted, the hotter her blood flamed for him.

Stripping in his bathroom was unbelievably erotic and her nipples peaked as she caught her image in the vanity mirror. She stepped into the tub and let it fill to her chin, sniffing the soap she'd taken from the plain white dish on the tub rim. She'd never wanted to lick soap before, but this smelled like him.

Turning the bar over in her palms, the aroma burst around her like a storm of desire, the bubbles sliding down her arms to her breasts. Rubbing the soap over her body was arousing and fired the need for sex in every part of her body.

Desire throbbed between her legs and she slid the soap down to press it to her pussy, drawing it up and down against her clit. Hard and slick, just the way he would be.

Damn it! She wasn't going to get herself off before he came upstairs. Waiting would only heighten the enjoyment of hearing him beg.

Chapter Four

Jack tried to forget Tessa, didn't want to think about her being upstairs, doing only Lord knew what.

He watched the weather, the sole story in town. Snow all night, snow all day tomorrow, and maybe a break the next day.

That meant he'd be holed up with a tiger for several days and she wasn't easy to live with. What on earth had possessed him, sent him running to bring her home like a kid after a stray puppy?

He'd known from day one she had her hooks into him. There simply hadn't been a time he could let it be known how hard he was for her, what with all her traveling and playboy escorts.

She'd sent out little signals that she was interested, giving him her best come hither smiles and on occasion, rubbing against him if the chance came about. But he wouldn't be second man on the totem pole. Only once had they had a few minutes alone, at a fancy cocktail party Drake had invited him to.

The crowd was noisy and getting loaded. He'd turned down enough hash to make a mint if he took it to the streets. All around him were red-faced sloppy men and skinny, high women. The scene was straight out of his college days.

He was getting ready to leave when out of the blue, Tessa was walking toward him. Alone, she'd been flirtatious and hot enough to melt his hair. One second away from him asking her for a date, her well oiled, model-looking date came to collect her.

That had been months ago. He'd learned a lot about her in that time, things he didn't want to know. She liked to party, sometimes drank too much, and ran with a well-heeled, anything goes crowd. She wouldn't give him the time of day and he didn't ask.

He yawned, tired of sitting downstairs and feeling too intimidated to go to his bedroom.

Hell with that, he was going to bed.

At the top of the stairs, he noticed that her door was open and the lights blazed.

He didn't care what she did as long as she was quiet about it. Maybe he should tell her goodnight, see if she needed anything.

Sucker. You haven't thought of anything but getting in bed with her. Ask for that.

He went to his room but left the door open in case she needed him. Jack couldn't believe his growing concern for Tessa. She'd rip his balls off just for laughs if the mood hit her.

After a quick shower, he dried in a hurry, glad to be home and out of the storm. He was accustomed to having the house to himself and walked around with no concern about being naked.

He reached for the switch on the bedside lamp, but her voice stopped him.

"I like the lights on."

He didn't grab his stuff or try to cover up. She had invaded his privacy. When he turned around, he saw Tessa wearing the thinnest champagne-colored gown he'd ever seen.

He didn't care if she saw his dick slap his belly. That's what she intended. "Tessa, I thought I made myself clear."

She was within reach but didn't touch him, releasing the laces that were crisscrossed over her full breasts. "You said no strings attached. I'm making sure."

He'd made that crazy statement, hadn't he?

"You're doing a good job, Tessa." He stood where he was, hands on his hips. "Damn good."

Hot blood thundered through his body, making him aware of her, not just that she was there, but the perfume in her hair, the pulse in her temple. He could feel the soft heat from her smooth skin, the slight tremble in her slender body.

She smiled the way he'd dreamed about, the kind that said she was wet for him.

Her fingers plucked the laces free, not reaching for the gown as it fell to the floor.

Jack forgot his naked body was laid bare for her to approve or disapprove. He didn't care if she just wanted sex. That's all he wanted. Lots of it.

She moved toward him with a teasing smile. "I've wanted this for a very long time, Jack."

He pulled her into his arms, wanting her with a hunger he'd pushed away for far too long. She sighed with a softness he'd never thought she possessed.

"You're so damn hot, Tessa." He lost all control of his tongue and cock while she plastered her slender body to him. "Are you wild cat or kitten tonight?"

For a fraction of a second, her tawny eyes narrowed. "If I don't come four times, I'm all tiger."

"Promises, promises." He picked her up and laid her on his bed. "Only four times?" He dropped onto the bed to gaze at her before pulling her arm around his neck.

She laughed her ball-squeezing laugh and touched his cock. "I'll be easy on you this time."

He was rock hard and her fingers on him shoved him toward climax. "I have a present for you, baby."

If he didn't pleasure her first, he wouldn't last through one stroke. She knew what he intended and relaxed her legs. Damn, he'd always imagined she'd have a sweet pussy, but his greed wouldn't let him admire the cake before he bent to taste it.

* * * *

His tongue barely touched her clit after he opened her wet folds to lick them slowly, driving her crazy with the occasional touch to her aching bud.

She tried to pull his face to her pussy, but he held her hand and went on with his torture. "I want it all...right now."

"You only get four chances, honey." He sat up and pulled her legs over his shoulders. He was smiling at her and she wanted to claw his hard-muscled belly. Sweet heaven, what was he doing to her?

He stroked her folds with his tongue, nipping her clit occasionally, each little nibble sending fire through her body.

Her heart skipped several beats while his long fingers stroked her into a fever pitch of need to be fucked. He didn't listen to her, went on with his maddening tease. She bucked her hips to take in his fingers, clenching around him to keep the delicious fire close.

She was so close to coming, yet he knew how to hold her off, burying his face between her legs to suck her pussy lips into his mouth. He pulled her clit between his teeth and bit, gently but enough to make her scream as the hot sizzles of fuck-me shot up her backbone.

She tried to sit up, reaching for his dick, but he took her hand and squeezed her fingers. "Are you ready for number one?"

"Yes, damn you." She was more than ready, wrapping her arms around his neck when he lay down to cover her trembling body. "Make me come, Jack."

His cock throbbed in her hand and she fantasized about the feel of it inside her. Large and hot, ridged with full veins and a slick head she wanted to taste.

His scent hypnotized her, drove her to the brink of sexual desire. Her lips swelled with the blood of passion, yielded to his closing over hers. His kiss was deep and searching, rough, sweet, and promising. She wanted him, wanted him inside her slick pussy and around her with his hard body.

The tip of his cock brushed her clit and she gasped, pulling down on his hips. Pleasure coursed through her, delicious quivers spiraling from her pussy to her mouth making her laugh with ecstasy.

He was solid, his olive body honed to perfection and he pumped like a well-oiled machine, driving deeper and harder, taking her out of reality. She rose up in flames, riding a wild wind and clinging to him to stay on earth.

"Jack…Jack…I'm coming...Jack!"

She dug her nails into the hard flesh of his ass while he thrust into her. The desire to never let him finish consumed her so much that her legs hugged his waist, his energy pulling her up to his belly.

This was what she wanted, being in bed with the man she couldn't win and could never forget.

No, remember he doesn't want you, he's only having sex with you.

God, she wanted him to desire her, but more than that, she wanted him to fall in love with her.

Chapter Five

"Something wrong, Tessa?" He slowed for a heartbeat to look into her eyes. "I can wait if you're not ready for number two." His voice was sexy, low, and gruff. "Tell me what you want, baby."

"I want to taste you." She'd never offered that to any man, but she wanted to have his full length in her mouth, to give him the kind of extreme pleasure he'd given her.

He rolled to his back, pulling her onto his belly. "Next time, gorgeous. Tonight is your party. At your mercy, Madame."

She liked the way he fisted her hair to draw her face close to his. "Your mouth is perfect." Kissing him made her gleefully happy, the firmness of his lips exciting and perfect. "It's too bad you waited so long to show me how delicious they are."

He stroked her back, and covered her mouth with his in a soft, searching kiss. "You're wrong, Tessa."

"What are you talking about?"

He shifted his position and rolled her onto her back. "You made me wait and enjoyed every second of it."

She knew what he meant. No need being honest just yet. "I think Jack needs to fuck me again." She inhaled deeply, wanting to cry with joy as he drove into her again.

This time, he didn't slow down or ask what she wanted, simply drove her into the second climax for the evening. When he came, he held her tight and cushioned her ass with his hands.

She still throbbed when he pulled from her and held her in his arms. "What's that smile for?" she asked.

He curled a strand of her hair around his finger, still smiling. "I've never seen you all fresh-fucked looking."

"Like it?" She was concerned that he found her unappealing now.

"Love it." He got out of bed to look out the window. "Want a drink?"

What should she say? He'd probably been told about her DUI and was testing her. "No thanks. You go ahead."

"I'll go get us a drink." He turned to smile at her and grabbed a blanket off the chair. "I don't like drinking alone."

While he was gone, Tessa freshened up in his bathroom. She was using his brush when he returned. "Hope you don't mind. I looked like a witch."

"Come back to bed and we'll mess it up again." He held two brandy snifters, waiting for her to join him. "I knew I was saving this for a special person."

There was no reason to refuse his hospitality. After all, they'd just had the best sex she'd ever experienced. "I'm glad to know I'm special to you, Jack."

She padded across the floor to crawl into the bed, still warm from their body heat. He joined her, propping her up against the pillows. She took the glass he held out and sipped the brandy. The brandy tasted excellent, just like him.

He swallowed a mouthful and leaned back, apparently content to have her in his bed. Several minutes passed before he spoke.

"You should be with your family."

He was speaking about his own desire to be where his family was, she thought. "Why on earth would I do that?" She tipped her glass to drain the contents.

He took the glass and eyed her with a hint of irritation. "What's with you and Drake? I know he's wondering where you are."

"That's a laugh." She sat up and glared at him. "What's it to you?"

"He's your family, Tessa."

"You want to hear about my family?" Here it came, questions and preaching from the one man she wanted no lecturing from. "My parents were old when I was born, completely in love with Drake and ignoring me. I had the misfortune of being a girl."

He took her hand. "All kids feel a little neglected if there are several." He probed deeper, and she suddenly remembered he was an attorney. "I'm sure they loved you. And Drake is hard to ignore."

"Yes, he is." She turned her head, not liking the conversation, but she couldn't stop. "They died when I was fifteen, within six months of each other."

His arm went about her waist. "I'm sorry. Want to talk about something else?"

"Sure." She drew the comforter up around them. "I went to college. Did Drake ever tell you that?"

Interest gleamed in his eyes and he leaned closer to gaze at her. "So, what did you study?"

"Art." She laughed at the idea that she'd really thought she was an artist. "I lasted two years."

"So, you're a college girl." He grinned, and she hoped he wasn't being condescending.

"No, I just spent time there. My brother gave the school a ton of money not to fail me." She was tired of the subject. "I simply dropped out."

The hug he gave her was like a warm lifeline.

Stop it, Tessa. He probably thinks you're a dumbass failure. And you are.

"Let's go downstairs and light my phony fireplace." He got up, pulling on a pair of gray sweatpants. "Here, put on my shirt."

"You don't want to look at my naked ass anymore?" She smiled, fastening the middle button.

"Not at all, I just know we'll wind up screwing on the stairs if you run around naked." He pulled her into his arms and pressed a soft kiss to her mouth. "I have a great couch."

His playful side came out as he led her downstairs to the living room. He picked her up and carried her to the bay window.

"What are you thinking, Jack?" She was curious about everything he thought or did.

"I was wondering if you'd like to build a snowman." He brushed her lips with his. "Maybe tomorrow."

He laid her on the comfortable couch, pressing her into the pillows. "Yes, maybe tomorrow." She loved his hands on her breasts and between her legs, flooded with desire as his weight held her willing prisoner.

She gave herself over completely to him, memorizing the strong contours of his back and the shape and texture of his lips. Flash fire whipped over her body while his tongue teased her nipples. She wanted more, holding back a scream while he drove her crazy.

Panic hit when he stood and ran up the stairs. "Jack!"

He reappeared, carrying the comforter from his bed. "That's what I like—an eager woman."

She wanted to yell at him, maybe hit him for leaving her at such a special moment. "What are you doing?"

"Lighting the fire." He knelt to turn on the electric flame and smiled at her. "It's for show only. Atmosphere."

She grabbed the comforter and spread it out in front of the fireplace. Still shaking with the lingering feeling of desertion, she lay down to gaze at him.

"I need you."

"Are you cold?" He lay down and covered her.

"I won't be when you light me up."

She wove her fingers deep in his hair, loving its cool crispness, glorying in the maleness of his body. He took her breath, playing with her clit until she was wet and grinding her hips against his hand.

He groaned, his breathing labored while she circled the head of his cock in her fingers, working him until he was as slick as her. She sat up, pushing him onto his back.

He tasted good, his tip large and a perfect fit for her mouth. The veins were engorged, his hot blood surging through them to make him hard as marble. She took in his entire length and sucked until he caught her face in his hands.

"That's so damn good, Tessa, but I want you to fuck me this time." His dark gaze locked with hers, and she almost came as he pulled her on top of him.

She moved up to straddle his hips, sliding forward to fit him into her wet pussy. The heat that blazed through her was unbearable, and she gripped him in a ferocious vise of passion-strengthened muscle. Her hips worked against his erection, furiously, while his cock strummed her clit with every motion. Fire built in her slit, ignited and burned out of control until she came in a shattering crimson inferno. His climax was powerful, delicious to watch while he gripped her shoulders and held her until he'd filled her with his juice.

They lay together for long moments, the calm after the storm taking away the earlier fury. Tessa yawned and kissed his chest. Life was suddenly good and she was happy for the first time in a very long time.

Chapter Six

"Want to share my hot bath?" Tessa flipped the warm, soapy water at him. God, she was unbelievable between the sheets. He couldn't get enough of her.

He finished shaving and dropped the towel that had hung from his waist. "You're too much, Tessa."

"Not for you." She leaned forward and made room for him behind her. "I'll wash your back if you'd like."

"Let's just relax for a minute." Jack thought over their all-night romp and had begun to regret being a horny fool.

He'd compromised his client-attorney relationship with Drake in a way that had no explanation. He'd asked him to take care of his sister, not fuck her brains out. Not that he hadn't gone to the moon with her. She was the most giving, sensual woman he'd ever slept with.

But she was volatile, and he knew she'd break his nose if he pissed her off. And there was also Link Griffin. He had no idea where that was going. Jack knew he was a fool of the worst kind.

"You're quiet, Jack." Her voice was calm, but her slender body stiffened against him. "What were you thinking?"

"A lady never asks a man something like that." He kissed her ear.

"As you know, I'm no lady." She turned to smile at him, and his gut wrenched in reaction to how beautiful she looked.

"You're perfect." He pulled her back to lie against him, trying to relax. He listened to the far off rumble of some kind of machinery and closed his eyes. He hadn't slept at all and it was catching up with him.

She sat forward and pointed to the door. "I hear something." He couldn't believe how fast she got out of the tub and grabbed several towels. "Link has sent them after me."

"Tessa." Damn if he could figure out why she was so scared of that punk. "I think it's a snowplow come to rescue us."

Her eyes were round and filled with fright. "Are you sure?"

"I hope the hell it is, so we can get something to eat." He remembered how afraid she'd looked at Griffin's apartment. "Let me worry about that bastard, okay?"

She clung to him for a moment, but quickly regained her tough exterior. "Want to have sex before breakfast?"

Jack saw no real desire in her eyes. It was obvious to him that she was trying to regain her "I don't give a damn" attitude. He didn't care to have sex with a woman trying to get even with some other guy.

"How about sex after breakfast?" The sweet smile she gave him said she was already aroused by the idea. "Let's get dressed and see what's open."

She kissed him, her tongue twisting around his while she rubbed his cock. "I'm ravenous."

"Me too, baby." Which was he hungrier for, eggs and bacon or her fine ass? The latter of course, but he had to have strength to give her what she wanted.

He followed her up the stairs, wanting to grab her and have a roll on the floor. She'd really gotten into his blood, and now he'd be lucky to ever get her out.

"I'll be ready in a flash." She patted his ass before disappearing into the room she was supposed to occupy.

"I'll be here." Why was he here? Just to sleep with a woman that wouldn't spit on him tomorrow.

While he pulled on jeans and boots, he could hear Tessa running water, closing doors. It all sounded good to him. He'd just finished buttoning his shirt when she stood in the door, watching him.

"I'm ready." She was a knockout in a black sweater and slacks that hugged her lush curves. "Is our car here yet?"

He had never known anyone so accustomed to being waited on. She didn't mean just a car, but one of her fleet. "Do you feel like digging my car out of two feet of snow?" He grinned, not surprised by the question in her eyes. "If you're wearing boots, we can walk to the café."

She looked down at her feet and held her coat out on her arm. "Will these do?"

"Yeah, they're boots all right." He shook his head, knowing the butter soft, high heeled boots wouldn't keep her feet warm. She looked so smug that he didn't say what he really thought. "Sure, they're perfect."

* * * *

"Whose big idea was this?" Tessa sat on her rear, brushing at the snow on her face. "I'm not that hungry."

Jack gripped her hand to pull her out of the snow bank she'd stumbled into. "That happens when the plow comes through."

She would have been angry, but he looked so damn good in his big old parka and cowboy boots. "Okay. Let's go." He kissed her hard, his firm lips warm on hers.

While they picked their way down the sidewalk, Tessa enjoyed the squeeze of his fingers on hers. She'd never had to walk anywhere and especially not in cold weather. Snowflakes drifted down again, and she didn't mind at all. She'd always hated winter, but that had been in the past.

She was with Jack now.

Another block and they reached the café he spoke of. The Blue Bird Bakery and Café was delightfully warm and the aromas made her mouth water.

He led her to the counter and took her coat to hang by the door. The rack was jammed with coats of the people who had gotten there earlier.

He rubbed his hands together and sat on the stool next to her. He immediately looked the menu over, licking his lips in anticipation. That could have been her reaction to him.

"Tessa, try the special." He put the menu back and spoke to the man beside him.

"Do you know everyone that comes in here?" She had noticed the pretty brunette waving at him and his smile at the woman.

"Pretty much." He gazed at her with a slow smile. "This is a small community of neighbors. That's what neighbors do. Speak to each other."

She was embarrassed, but Tessa wasn't buying that he only spoke to this woman. Jealousy was a new emotion to her. "If you say so, and I'll have the special."

"Great." He gave their order to the busy waitress and sipped his coffee.

His cell played something western and she hid her smile. Her Wild-West man had to give in to modern annoyances too. He kissed her cheek and walked to the bakery display to talk.

Curiosity was eating her up about Jack's personal life. At least he had one. His expression said he wasn't pleased with what the other person was saying. Oh God, it couldn't be Drake ruining things again.

His mood had done an about-face by the time he sat beside her.

"Has something happened?" She had to know or have a breakdown. "Was that Drake?"

"No." He waited for the waitress to place their meal in front of them and walk away. "Nothing for you to worry about. Eat your breakfast."

Okay, she had been nosy, and he didn't like it. Just one more thing she'd learned about him.

He didn't eat like a man who was hungry. He looked preoccupied and kept glancing at the door. Now she was scared. "What's going on? That phone call was about me, wasn't it?"

He handed her the small cream pitcher and pulled his expression into a smile. "Enjoy those eggs and ham. We may have to walk back here for lunch."

"I don't care about breakfast or lunch." The woman that had smiled at him earlier stared at her as if she were raping him. She scowled at her, silently telling her to mind her own business. "Link knows where I am."

He gripped her arm. "Calm down. We're not leaving until you eat something, okay?"

Fear closed her throat, and she choked on a bite of eggs. She waved off his hand that slapped her on the back several times. Okay, she could do this. She'd been in tougher spots. One, two, three, swallow the toast. The coffee washed it down and she looked at him, freezing the fear in her chest.

"I'm finished." She grabbed her coat and headed for the door. "I'll wait outside."

"No." He tossed several bills on the counter and motioned her to the bakery display case.

She couldn't believe he was buying sweets when she was facing Link's wrath. She stood beside him and smiled at the counter girl with stiff lips, finally able to choose what she wanted from the display. "I don't like those things with jelly in them. I like cream horns."

"What is a cream horn?" He looked in the case and pointed to the long johns. "No jelly, okay?"

"Whatever the hell you want." She shrugged on her coat and peered out the fogged up windows.

He picked up his parka and took the sack that the clerk placed on the counter. "Are you okay?" He followed her out the door. "Come on. Let's take the shortcut."

His shortcut was a landmine of drifts and ice that had him half carrying her back to the house. He didn't say much, just scared her to death with his constant surveillance of anything that moved in the silent streets.

She was breathless when he finally opened his door and ushered her inside.

"Stop lying to me." She flung her coat to the floor and held his arm. "I'm not stupid, so stop treating me that way."

"You're going to have to settle down." He laid his coat on a chair. "By the time Dresslehouse gets here, I want you speaking coherently and without that rage in your voice."

"I knew it." Her voice squeaked and her hands shook. "They are arresting me for breaking Link's nose."

He pulled her close and smoothed her hair. "No, this is a lot more serious."

"What else could there be?" She began to tremble uncontrollably.

"He's dead."

Chapter Seven

How long would they have to wait on that son of a bitch Dresslehouse? Tessa drank the last of the scotch and stared out the window, looking small and defenseless, hugging herself as if to ward off evil.

It was late and the sun was setting. Hiding his nervousness from her was impossible. She jumped at every sound and watched him for his reaction. He didn't blame her for being worried.

They were in a situation that was as serious as a heart attack.

He pulled the cord on the plantation blinds, and they clattered to the floor. Tessa screamed and jumped as if the roof had fallen in on them. For her sake, he had to get his shit together. She was scared enough without him stumbling around like a wild boar.

He smiled at her and pushed the blinds aside to look out the window for the tenth time. Heavy snow had begun to fall again and Jack was sweating.

Had something been found that meant they could be taken into custody? It couldn't be. They hadn't left the house in twenty-four hours.

"You have to believe this won't touch you." Jack kissed her cheek, taking the empty glass from her hand. Worry seeped up his spine when the doorbell chimed softly. Her eyes filled with fear. "That will be Dresselhouse."

"Don't leave me alone with them, please." She grabbed his hand, worry etching her forehead. "What if they arrest me?"

"You haven't done anything. You have nothing to worry about." Jack didn't want her harassed or taken to the stinking jail downtown. "They'll leave soon."

He opened the door, facing Dresslehouse and his partner. He had never gotten used to the man's height and weightlifter's build.

"Can we come in, Savage?"

Did he have a choice? Not really. "Sure. Come on in."

Tessa stood by the fireplace, eyeing the two newcomers with hard suspicion. He took her arm and guided her to the kitchen.

"Might as well have coffee while we talk."

The two detectives followed him, sitting down at the table to take out their notebooks and pens. They smiled at Tessa when she sat down as close to the door as possible.

"Okay, gentlemen, let's get started." Jack wasn't as composed as he sounded. He chose a chair next to Tessa and sipped the warmed-up coffee that tasted like mud.

"Ms. Duval, where were you last night?" Dresselhouse gazed at her with no emotion showing.

"I was here." She chose the best answer she could have.

"All night?"

"Yes." She lost her composure. "How did he die…I mean, was he in an accident?"

Jack spoke up, wanting her to say as little as possible. "We came straight here after I talked to you."

Taking a slow look around the kitchen, the second detective made notes and twirled his pen at Jack. "You have a weapon, Savage?"

"I do, all registered and clean."

"Where is it?"

"In the desk."

"Get it, please." Jack went to his desk and pulled the pistol from its holster. He handed it to Dresselhouse and observed the detective as he sniffed the barrel and flipped the chamber open. "You ought to clean this thing sometime." He put the gun back in the drawer. "Don't look so worried. Griffin was killed with a forty-five."

"I wasn't worried, just waiting for you guys to leave." Jack hid the deep breath he sucked in, relieved they weren't going to lineup.

Tessa had tears in her eyes and slumped in her chair. She jumped when Dresselhouse spoke directly to her. "You know who his enemies were? Would one of your friends take him out?"

Her eyes widened in surprise. "Of course I don't know. He wasn't in that type of crowd." She looked like a scared rabbit. "None of my friends have guns."

"That's good." He nodded. "Did you know he was gay?"

"He was bisexual, not gay."

Jack bit his tongue. "If you guys have all you need, I think Tessa needs to relax."

"Just need to get a line on the hours after you left Griffin's apartment." The quiet detective poised his pen over the notebook.

"I picked up Tessa at Griffin's place at five-thirty, called you before we left." Jack kept it simple. Fewer words meant fewer mess ups. "I dropped her off at her place at six. Because she seemed scared of what Griffin might do, I went back to her home and brought her here. That was around six-thirty."

"And you were here all night? Didn't go out?" Dresselhouse obviously needed convincing.

"Did you notice the blizzard that came through here last night?"

"Right." After glancing at Tessa, Dresselhouse rose and headed for the door. "I don't have to remind you to stick around town, do I counselor?"

"I'm not going anywhere." Jack cursed himself for not sticking with his original plans to go home. But that was hindsight. He was responsible for Tessa now, and she needed him.

He closed the door and locked it after the detectives left.

"I want to go home." Tessa stood and tried to go up the stairs.

"Why?" Jack followed her, wanting to reassure her that there was no reason to run. "You can stay here as long as you want."

She gazed at him like she had in the past, cool and distant. "Go ahead and ask."

"What are you talking about?" He scraped his hand over his face. Why couldn't she be straight with him?

"Griffin and I never had sex." She hesitated, as if she didn't want to reveal any more about her life. "I was in love once, last year. He was an artist I met in college. He didn't suit Drake's standards, and after paying my friend a lot of money, he left."

"You didn't lose much then." Jack corrected the callous statement. "You surely realize he wasn't as deeply involved as you were."

"Yes, I know that now." She went to the window and then turned to face him. "Link and I used each other for appearances. If I wanted to party, he'd go with me, and I did the same for him." She tucked her hair behind her ear. "Is that what you wanted to hear?"

"It's none of my business." He wasn't about to tell her how glad he was that relationship had been nothing. "But I would like to know why you let him beat around on you."

She huffed softly. "I did my share of hurting him. I'd gotten fed up with his increased drinking binges and drugs. I told him that yesterday when he hit me and I retaliated."

"Do you still want to go home?" He didn't want her to leave, not yet. "Wait until morning, okay?"

She nodded and put her arms around his neck. "I hoped you'd say that."

He should have shoved her into a cab that first day and slammed the door behind the queen of trouble, but how could he do that to the woman that melted his heart with her slightest glance? He hoped she wanted to stay with him, not because she was afraid, but because she wanted him.

* * * *

Tears rolled down her cheeks and she hid her face against his shoulder. He didn't ask questions, just held her tight until she stopped crying.

"Better now?" He stroked her hair and kissed her. "I'll do anything you want."

"I want to go to his funeral."

"Griffin's funeral?"

"Yes. He was my friend."

Jack exhaled and gazed down at her. "That is not a good idea."

"Why?"

He shook his head and looked at her with a tinge of anger in his eyes. She didn't have to hear what he thought. His hard gaze spoke all too clearly. He seemed to know everything about her, knew about all the times Link had pushed her around, left her waiting for him in front of bars while he shot up with drugs and her screaming at him to stop doing those things.

"Okay, Tessa." He raked fingers through his hair. "I'll go with you."

He took her breath with his constant consideration. "I'd like that." She hugged him, wishing the warmth between them would never fade.

"It's seven o'clock, Tessa, but the café is still open." He kissed her slowly, gently. "You get comfortable, and I'll go hunt down something to eat."

"You heard my stomach growl." She laughed at her own words. "I love being with you." She hated the loneliness that fell upon her after he let her go. Hungry or not, she didn't want him to leave her. "I'll go too."

"No." He buttoned his parka and grabbed his gloves, finishing his comment on the small porch. "I'm taking the shortcut, and you didn't do too well in that alley if I remember right." He dropped a quick kiss on her lips. "Go inside and lock the door. I'll be back soon."

She took up her watch for his return in the window seat overlooking the homes across the street. Gaily lit Christmas trees could be seen in most of the windows.

She watched a young couple across the street shoveling snow from their driveway. They were laughing, throwing snowballs at each other, happy and in love.

What would it be like to have that, a true love? Maybe with Jack? Fool, you have blown that with your easy sex and don't-give-a–damn-about-anything attitude.

She sighed heavily, lonely and confused. Two days ago she was buying a mink coat and a diamond bracelet at her favorite shop on the Plaza.

Today, here she sat in a virtual stranger's home with nothing but the memory of the best sex she'd ever had.

Glancing out at the evening darkness, she reached for her handbag and pulled out her cell phone. After hitting speed dial, her brother's voice came on the phone.

"Drake." She hesitated. "I have something to tell you."

There was the usual moment of silence on his end of the line. "Merry Christmas, Tessa." His laugh was dry and short. "What kind of trouble are you in now?"

There was no easy way to say it. "Link is dead and I am staying with Jack." There, she'd gotten the worst part out. "I'm going to the funeral and Jack is going with me."

"Unbelievable." Drake sounded angry, and it chilled his voice. "I forbid it." She heard him take in a deep breath before he continued. "I've asked you to give up that crowd for years. It's a wonder you haven't spent some time in jail because of your refusal to act like an adult."

She let the barb go uncontested. "The police questioned me and Jack." Now it was Drake's turn to wait for more information.

"What the hell? Tessa!" She figured his face was turning red while his blood pressure rose. "You didn't tell me why they questioned you. Was Link murdered? Spill it all. Right now."

"I am not under suspicion. Link was alive when I last saw him. Plus, I have been with Jack." She couldn't help the wry grin that touched her lips. "All night."

"God help the man."

Chapter Eight

Jack couldn't shake the nagging knot of worry in his gut. Tessa was determined to be at Link's funeral.

What a weekend. He had learned more than he wanted to know about the Duval family. The woman he'd wanted from afar had moved in and taken over his life and heart. He was well aware that he was crazy about the combustive beauty, but knew not to make plans for anything permanent.

While she spoke to the funeral director of the funeral home where Link had been taken, Jack sat on her bed listening to her side of the conversation. While she spoke to the funeral director where Link was laid out, Jack sat on her bed. She smiled his way and scribbled something on a fancy notepad.

Astounding woman. He splits her lip and she's sending flowers.

"What's wrong?" Tessa hung up the phone and gazed at him. She pushed a strand of hair away from her cheek. "You think I'm crazy, don't you Jack?"

"No." He held his hands out to squeeze her fingers. "I know you're a beautiful, caring woman."

Her arms went around his neck as she sat on his lap. "You make me so happy. I'm not afraid anymore."

He leaned back to study her face. "What were you afraid of?"

"Being alone and never finding you."

Okay. She was doing exactly what he didn't want. Mistaking tenderness and good sex for love. She assumed he wanted to make this a full time thing and it was his fault. He did want that. That would be great, except she'd probably dump him in a New York minute if she decided he wasn't what she wanted.

"Tessa." He moved her onto the bed and rose, bothered by the disappointment in her eyes. "You have way too much to offer someone to not look around before settling on a guy you hardly know."

Her lashes lowered, shielding any emotion she felt, but he heard it, no matter how modulated her reply. "I thought we understood each other, Jack." She rose and began taking her clothes off. "I said you made me happy, not that you were anyone I'd want to keep around."

Why couldn't he keep his mouth shut? She had that same closed expression he'd assumed was her normal look before seeing her heartbreaking smile.

"Do you want me to stay tonight?"

"No, I don't need the distraction."

"From what?" He really was curious about her plans. "Don't try to drive. The streets are still slick."

She rolled her eyes and removed her earrings, tossing the four carat diamonds on the bedside table. "I have a driver."

He wanted to stay, but that wasn't a good idea. They would probably have another argument and he was in no mood for it. He wanted to stay, but it wouldn't be pleasant. He was still worried about her safety. Her chin set in a stubborn line that meant there was no changing her mind.

"I'll be there, Tessa." He paused at the writing desk on the way out of her bedroom to pick up the note pad. "Come down and lock the door, okay?"

She got up to follow him down the stairs. "You don't have to come, you know. Drake said he was flying in tomorrow morning."

Jack took a ragged breath. He was glad Drake was coming home. Maybe he could change her mind about attending the funeral.

"Tessa, you know there will be news crews and more cops than you've ever seen." He turned the doorknob, waiting for her to say something. "You are still considered a person of interest. Do you want the publicity?"

She moved his hand and opened the door wide. "I'm used to it, Savage." She pointed to the walkway. "I won't use your name if that's what you're worried about."

He knew he'd made the right decision. They were as different as salt and pepper. "Lock the door."

Damn! Why hadn't he gone on with his life instead of letting her mess him up like a jigsaw puzzle? It would have been so simple, get on that plane and forget her and that dead son of a bitch.

Jack pulled into a fast food place parking lot. He groaned, letting the truth sink in.

It would all be here when you got back, the snow, the job, and you would bust your balls to see Tessa again.

That revelation wasn't new to him, and Jack had thought about it with regular frequency. No amount of sex would make them breathe the same air or want the same life. She was Tessa, multi-million-dollar heiress, and he was average Joe and liking it.

Get out now, Savage. She flies too high for your simple taste.

* * * *

He thought she was crazy.

And now he'd told her in his smooth attorney style that he was finished being her boyfriend.

Tessa thought about the way she'd fallen for all his rancher boyish charm, even spent insane moments feeling that she'd found Mr. Right. The only thing right about Jack was his expertise in bed.

That's a lie. He's strong and kind and all the things you've never seen in a man before.

Looking around her apartment, she knew the silence would drive her crazy if she stayed home.

Hell with this.

Grabbing her coat and purse from the chair where she'd dropped it, Tessa hurried out the door to find the comfort of music, laughter, and her unpredictable friends.

Not wanting to risk her driver's habit of spying on her and reporting back to Drake, she backed her red sports car from the garage. The ice on the driveway only briefly concerned her.

She managed to drive away from her complex and head for the loudest bar in Westport. No one there would give a damn about her private life or what she did with it.

Tessa swiped a hand at the tears blurring her vision.

She wasn't a crybaby, but right now, her heart was breaking and she couldn't stop them from streaming down her cheeks.

She saw the red light and hit her brakes, but her car skidded on through the intersection, sliding to a stop after crashing into a mailbox on the sidewalk.

The airbag inflated with mind-boggling speed and force. A few seconds passed before the pain in her nose and cheekbones set in, and she screamed in the aftershock of being jolted forcefully in a blink of an eye.

Too shaken to remove the seatbelt, she wept in frustration.

People rushed to the car and knocked on the window, yelling at her to see if she was all right.

She struggled to open the door and tried to get out.

"Why don't you stay put, lady? Your nose is bleeding."

The earnest words from a skinny kid in a skull cap and fleece jacket sobered Tessa. She lifted her hand to touch her nose, drawing it back when pain shot through her again.

Fresh tears rolled down her numb face when she witnessed the blood on her hand.

Her phone. Where was her phone?

The concerned kid opened her door and reached across her lap to grab her purse and hand it to her. "Want me to dial for you?"

She shook her head and took the cell phone he'd taken out of her handbag. "No…no thanks. I can do it." She tried to smile, but her lips seemed frozen in a grimace.

Tessa punched in the number of the one person she wanted to see. When the phone rang and he said hello, her heart pounded with frantic relief.

"Jack." Fresh tears streamed down her face once again. "I need you."

Chapter Nine

After talking with the kid who had obviously taken over at the scene, Jack tried to calm his heartbeat down to a sane level.

Tessa! He hadn't been surprised, just worried to hell about her. He backed out of the garage and skidded down the sloping driveway, wondering what on earth had possessed Tessa to drive on a night like this.

Jack promised himself he'd choke her if and when he ever got to St. Luke's Hospital.

Thirty white-knuckled minutes later, he hurried into the emergency room where he was directed to a curtained off alcove.

His gut knotted in shock when he saw Tessa propped up against pillows, her nose packed with gauze and both eyes circled in dark blue.

He wondered if the nurses had asked about the older bruise on her cheek.

Damn. She looked pitiful, and all he wanted to do was hold her.

She finally noticed him standing in the doorway and began to cry.

"Tessa." He couldn't believe she was so upset, the girl that had been slapped around by a jerk and fought the world with no help or complaint. He moved to the head of the gurney to lean over her. "How's my girl?"

She sat up to hug him, her slender body quaking with sobs. "I'm so glad you came. Thank you."

For several minutes, he held her, listening to her account of what happened. "I should be mad as hell at you, Tessa, but I'm just grateful you weren't badly hurt."

She covered her nose with her hand. "I must look horrible." Looking at him with a puffy-lipped smile, Tessa waited for his answer.

"You're gorgeous no matter what." He meant that, seeing past the bruises and gauze sticking out of her nose. "I'll take you home and stay with you." He qualified his meaning. "For tonight. That is, if you don't mind. I'd like to make sure you're all right."

"No." She pulled the sheet up to cover her nose and mouth.

"Why not?" Her stubborn, inconsistent personality pissed him off.

"You weren't worried about me earlier. Anyway, I need to be alone." She wiped her eyes with the sheet bunched in her hand. "And if you can't stay more than a few hours, I'd just as soon you didn't come at all. I'll call James to come for me."

That idea irked Jack. "Will James undress you and put you in bed?" He pulled her hands away from her face. "Who the hell is this James character?"

He couldn't believe his ears. She laughed, or more like giggled. She held his hand and relaxed against the pillows.

"My Jack is jealous." Her yawn meant the pain relievers were kicking in. "I love you, Jack."

God help him, he had to say it. "And I love you, Tessa."

He sat by her bed while the nurse checked Tessa's vital signs, and the intern looked her over one final time. Armed with medication and instructions on keeping Tessa warm and quiet, Jack once again took on full responsibility for her care.

In the car, she leaned against him and smiled at everything he said. This night, he would take care of her and try to figure out what came next. Tomorrow, he would put her in the hands of her brother.

Thirty minutes later, Tessa had been tucked into her bed where she promptly fell asleep. Jack turned up the thermostat and crashed on the fancy white couch. Unlike the princess in the bedroom, he couldn't fall asleep. The drone of the television helped some, but the weather report was lousy.

More snow coming tomorrow night and he could have been in sunny Arizona. He turned off the set and lay down on the couch, trying to get comfortable. Arizona would always be there.

* * * *

Her body ached some, but Tessa couldn't be concerned about a little pain, not after she got a look at her swollen lips and the blue circles around both eyes.

Jack. The aroma of coffee brewing meant he'd stayed the night. She got out of bed and hurried into the bathroom. Come hell or high water, she wouldn't let him see her looking like a prize fighter.

She worked quickly, disguising the discoloration framing her eyes with eye shadow, lots of mascara and a double slathering of foundation. Pale pink lipstick wouldn't draw attention to her mouth. She eyed her reflection with a hard grimace of disgust. She looked like hell.

The doorbell rang, her stomach knotting with apprehension. That had to be Drake, and she prayed he'd come alone. She had no desire to see anyone else.

She pulled on a pair of beige slacks and a white sweater, combing her hair into a casual loose style. If she leaned forward a lot, her bruises wouldn't be too noticeable.

Idiot. Just face up to it.

At the top of the stairs, she could hear Drake's commanding voice and Jack's softer drawl. She went downstairs, taking deep breaths, struggling to force a smile on her lips.

Both men stood near the fireplace, having a cup of coffee like two old cronies. They both looked at her, Drake with his usual accessing gaze and Jack with a warm smile on his handsome face.

"Drake, I hope you didn't have any problem getting here." Surprised by her ability to sound calm, Tessa went to him, hugging his waist. "I'm sorry for ruining your holiday."

She wanted to lean on him and cry her eyes out, but she couldn't. Jack didn't comment, but brought the coffee urn to the living room and poured her a cup.

He didn't appear to be ill at ease or worried. She loved him for sticking around and grabbed his hand when he started to leave the room.

Drake sat on the couch, eyeing the folded blanket and pillow. He didn't appear to be too angry, but she knew he had a big spiel to unload on her. He leaned toward her, obviously preparing his speech.

"Tess, how many more scrapes are you planning to get into?" He carefully placed his cup on the coffee table. "Savage filled me in on the situation and we both owe him a great deal." Drake's blue eyes pierced her defensive shield. They always did.

"It just happened, Drake." She shifted in her chair. "I'm not in trouble, and Jack will take me to the funeral."

"What?" Drake glared at her, meaning he hadn't finished raking her over the coals. "Of all the asinine ideas, that takes the prize." He pointed his finger at her. "You are not going. That's out."

"Yes, I am." Tessa conjured up the will to stand her ground. "You have no right to come here and throw your weight around." She liked his expression of disgust. Just like always, he tried to think of something to threaten her with.

"Tessa." Drake used his best calm, parental tone. "Think of your name, your family. Not only is this Link person an unsavory type, but he has been murdered. This isn't a normal funeral. You can't do this. I won't allow it."

He'd thrown the gauntlet down and she picked it up. "You can go home, Drake. I'll go because he would show me the same respect." She went to the door and waited for him to follow her.

Jack stepped in, putting on his coat. "I'll take her. It's important to Tessa, and I can't see the harm in it."

Drake shook his head, capitulating to defeat. "We've imposed on you enough, Savage. It's only proper that I take her. I'll take her."

Tessa stopped Jack before he could slip out the door, pulling his coat together while she smiled at him. "Thank you, Jack. For being my friend."

To her surprise, he kissed her on the lips. He grinned and grazed his finger over her chin. "Hope that didn't hurt."

She handed him the gloves he'd dropped on the hall table the night before. "You'd never hurt me."

Tessa watched him clear the windshield of his car and returned his wave as he drove off down the snow-packed street.

Loneliness swept over her, his leaving reinforcing the growing need to be with him concealed deep in her heart.

Chapter Ten

What a perfect day for a funeral. Jack couldn't believe he would be spending the better part of his Wednesday there considering that when the jerk was alive, he'd strutted around, hitting Tessa.

He looked out the bedroom window to see a world transformed into a blast of sunshine. The craziest weather he'd ever seen, but he'd begun to like it.

He dreaded going to the funeral, but he'd told her he'd be there. He felt a twinge of guilt, regretting being the hero, telling Drake he would drive Tessa to the service. The responsibility of seeing that Tessa got there was now his. He sure as hell didn't want her driving anymore until the spring thaw.

What a woman. One minute she was petty and childish, the next warm and all woman. He had tried to convince himself that he didn't give a rat's behind what she did. Lies, all lies. He did care and she'd worked her way into his every thought.

It wouldn't do though. Her world spun in a different orbit. He didn't party with crowds of strangers, didn't throw money around like rice at a wedding. He had plans, to make a success of his law firm, to marry one day and have kids. His plans did not include worrying about the vixen with blonde hair.

He grimaced, seeing that it was time to head for the service being held for Link.

He left the calm sanctuary of his home and drove toward Tessa's townhouse apartment. At least the streets were not icy and the sky had cleared. He glanced at his watch, making a bet with himself that she wouldn't be ready when he got there.

Jack knew he spent far too much time thinking about Tessa. It had been that way from the first time he'd seen her. She had seemed like a lost waif until he'd witnessed the first of several screaming matches between her and Drake.

He'd tried to steer clear of her, but it seemed Ms. Tessa always mysteriously showed up at her brother's office every time he did. Whether it happened by design or just plain bad luck, he didn't know.

Now he found his ass in a trap set by his own stupidity…or his lack of control.

He parked in front of Tessa's townhouse apartment, surprised to see her come out and lock the door. She looked as if she should be going to a photo shoot instead of burying some goofball. Tessa being Tessa, she had dressed in a full-length black mink and a wide-brimmed hat with wispy plumes around the crown. Her large rimmed black sunglasses completed the look.

He opened the door and she climbed in. "Seat belt, Tessa."

"Good morning to you, too."

"Are you feeling up to this?" He didn't comment on the bruises on her face. She'd done a good job of using foundation, but he could see the tint of blue under the makeup.

She checked her appearance in a gold compact and fussed with her hat before acknowledging him. "More than up to it." She crossed her legs and leaned back with a sigh. "I need to talk seriously with you."

Jack had doubts about the seriousness of the conversation. What did they ever talk about? "No time better than the present, Tessa."

"You're planning to never see me again, aren't you?"

"Tessa." He thought about pulling off the road to answer her. "Can't this wait until later?"

"I take that as a yes."

Maybe he should tell her she was right, that he didn't want to be in the middle of her mach-speed life. Jack shook his head, frustration needling him into being short with her. "Drop it, Tessa. Let's just get this freak show over with before we tackle your needs."

Instead of looking hurt or angry, she pulled the collar of her coat closer to her face and stared ahead. Apparently, she had gone back into "Tessa the bitch" mode with no problem.

He sensed her riveting gaze and knew she had something nasty to say. "I have to tell you something before Drake talks you into proposing to me."

He did a double take. "Say what?"

"Oh yes, I know he likes you. He's hinted enough times that we would be good for each other." She snorted in a most unladylike fashion. "He didn't mean in bed."

"Hell, Tessa." Jack swallowed against his dry throat. "What's that got to do with anything? Say what you're going to say."

"Don't be scared." She worked her leather gloves off. "I would never marry you. You're low class and ignorant. Plus, you're impoverished."

"Gee, that's a load off my mind." If he hadn't found her words amusing, he'd have been pissed off. "Thanks for letting me off the hook."

What had she expected? Knowing the woman even as little as he did, she looked damn irritated by his thoughts on the subject.

"Savage, the minute the funeral service is over, you get out of my life." Tessa clamped her lips tight, but he knew tears when he saw them.

A clump of snow falling from an overhead branch startled her. She leaned against him and shivered.

"You'll be okay, Tessa. And I'll miss you."

* * * *

Why had she said all that to Jack? Tessa wanted to spend every second with him, and yes, she wanted to marry him.

She had to regain her cool way of treating men, especially Jack. That was a dumb thought. After today, he'd do everything possible to stay away from her. Oh God, that hurt.

She slanted a quick glance his way. What if he left for Arizona? The thought of never seeing him again sat like a cold stone on her heart.

No more time to worry about that. The funeral home loomed up like a warning of ugly things to come. Added to the gloomy atmosphere, Drake stood outside, obviously waiting to make sure she didn't do something to embarrass him.

He opened the car door for her and wore his grim "I'm watching you" look.

"Tessa." He nodded to Jack and guided her into the chapel. "Let's get this over with."

She didn't feel like causing a scene. Not today. Her life would be like a never-ending funeral if she never saw Jack again.

Drake put his arm around her, showing support even though she knew he wanted to strangle her. She smiled at him, a rush of happiness warming her at being with her brother. Tessa wanted their relationship to be like this all the time. Maybe if she could stop being herself, it could happen.

Jack waited until she sat down and took the seat beside her. She took off her sunglasses and dropped them in her handbag. Drake glanced her way with a shrug.

Tears welled in her eyes. She'd forgotten her black eyes and swollen nose. Her own brother found her disgusting. "I'm sorry, Drake."

He put his arm across her shoulders. "For what? I'm grateful you're all right."

She dabbed her eyes with a tissue and put the sunglasses back on. "Thank you."

Jack took her hand, his attention on several large men stationed at a side door. She recognized the tallest man. Detective Dresslehouse.

As if sensing her worry, Jack reassured her. "He's just checking the crowd out. It's normal."

"Oh, I didn't know."

"He may want to speak with me later. Don't worry."

"I owe you an apology too, Jack." She loved his lifted brow and half smile. "I ruined your Christmas."

"Listen, Tessa." He leaned close to her, his cologne teasing her memory. "I want to make sure you are going to be okay. If you need me later on, just call me. Let's just get this behind us."

Her heart broke completely in two, the finality of his words cutting deep. He didn't want her, didn't say he wanted to hear from her. Worst thing of all, she knew he used that same line on all his clients.

"I won't bother you, Jack." She'd never been more determined about anything in her life. She would win him heart and soul, no matter what it took. "Help me with my coat, please."

He didn't say a word as her mink slid off her arms, but simply grinned and shook his head. Drake scowled and tapped his finger on her arm.

"Tessa, for God's sake. Had you nothing else to wear?" Her brother had been the poster boy for propriety all his life. "A tomato-red dress?"

She shrugged, straightened the long sleeve of the red knit dress and looked straight ahead. "He would have liked it."

Tessa knew keeping his voice low when he was furious cost Drake a lot emotionally. He tried to pull her coat around her shoulders, growling under his breath.

"Why do you have to be a freaked out rebel every day?" He flushed to his scalp with frustration. "You take great pride in dishonoring your family's name. I'm through trying to tell you anything. Go your way."

Her heart lurched with surprise. Drake had said that same thing to her more than once, but this time he meant it. His normally quiet expression had set in a cold frown.

So far, Jack hadn't reacted to her choice of outfits. He carefully kept his gaze on the proceedings at the front of the chapel. She sighed, secretly wishing she'd dressed in something appropriately dark and drab.

She put on her coat and stared at the line of mourners threading past the coffin. She didn't know any of them. That's all she had in her life—strangers wanting to have a drink and then on their way to be with their real friends.

This wasn't what she wanted. What she wanted sat next to her, and if she had to beg him, Jack would never shut her out of his life.

After the service concluded, Tessa took Jack's arm as they left the building. Drake tucked her under his shoulder and kissed her cheek.

"I'm sorry, Tessa."

She smiled at him, grateful that at least he was still speaking to her. "It's all right, Drake. I'll see you soon."

Drake walked away then to go to his car, leaving her alone with the man she would have to fight for. Jack turned his collar up and tightened his grip on her arm.

She froze as Dresslehouse approached them, his large frame casting a shadow over her. He spoke to Jack and nodded in her direction.

"Just thought you'd both want to know that we have Griffin's killers in custody." He chewed his gum for a second and went on. "It turned out to be a carjacking gone sour. Random thing. Just thought you'd want to know you're both cleared." He grinned. "Want to make a bet this isn't the last time we have a chat?"

Jack grimaced. "We weren't worried. But thanks for making it official." He groaned as a pack of reporters ran toward them. "Let's get out of here."

Being hounded by the press wasn't new to Tessa. From fifteen on, she'd been in the headlines for everything from bungee jumping off the busiest bridge in Kansas City to snowballing the mayor's car.

Tessa leaned against Jack, not for safety, but to make sure they were seen as a couple. "I'm scared, Jack."

"That will be the day." He practically carried her to his car and opened the door, waiting for her to fasten her seatbelt.

She watched him as he walked around to get in the driver's seat and turn the key in the ignition. His gaze never turned to her, his way of telling her they were finished.

That's what you think, my love.

Chapter Eleven

He had the office to himself that Saturday, and Jack rolled his sleeves up, prepared to catch up on the work he'd been putting aside.

The date on the desk calendar reminded him he'd been in a private hell for three months. February and the elm trees outside his windows had sprouted their buds.

He'd tried to go back to being all business and even put off going home until spring. Well, spring lurked just around the corner and he still had no desire to leave town.

The bottle of whiskey his best friend had sent as a Christmas gift caught his attention. Drinking alone brought him no pleasure, but right now he didn't much care.

He poured three fingers in a glass and took a long sip, arching his brows with approval. His friend knew quality. His choice of wife proved that. Not to mention the two kids and custom built mansion he lived in.

He shook off the wandering thoughts and sat down at his desk. His girl Friday could type like a tornado, but her handwriting looked like pure hieroglyphics.

One more reason for him to pack it in and head for his apartment.

He rose and stretched, reaching for his coat, the sudden turning of the door handle startling him. He paused before deciding to see which client showed up on the wrong day. A little pissed, he unlocked the door and swung it open.

"Tessa."

His heart thundered and his belly knotted as he looked into her beautiful dark eyes.

"Jack." She smiled at him, motioning to the interior of his office. "Are you alone?"

Tessa being polite? His curiosity piqued.

"Yes," he answered, feeling clumsy after almost stumbling over his feet to let her inside. "Of course. Come in."

"Surprised?" She turned to watch him close the door.

"You could say that." His soft laugh was due to the blast of shock her arrival had sent through him. "Kind of like waking up with your face sewn to the carpet."

She nodded and went to the window. "I remembered your birthday."

He thought about the cards from his family, the box of homemade cookies and new shirts his mother had sent. But here in his office stood the one gift he wanted most and felt such confusion about.

He didn't touch her, stood with his hands in his pockets, waiting. "What have you been doing these past weeks?"

Her smile when she looked his way could only be described as wistful. "I'm back in school. Making something of myself as Drake said."

Jack warmed to the idea. "That's great, Tessa." He poured two cups of coffee from the urn that he'd filled earlier and held one out to her. "Is it art still?"

"No." She sipped her coffee and moved toward his desk. "I'm studying for a degree in social services."

He choked on the hot coffee. "Social services?"

She put her cup on a bookcase and leaned on the desk, looking demure as hell.

"Come here, Jack." She crooked her dainty finger at him in a beckoning waggle. Her shoulder relaxed and he caught a glimpse of creamy sweet flesh under the collar of her coat. "I want to wish you a proper happy birthday."

Not go? Don't be a fool. She's all you want.

She sat on the edge of the desk, slowly swinging her leg in an enticing circle. His body reacted to the way she opened her legs in invitation. Hard. He'd become mahogany and his blood pounded hot with weeks of denial.

"Tessa, my sexy little fox." Nothing could keep him from her now, not now. She played him like a drum, slow and deep, letting the coat open to fall in rich folds around her bare hips. The rosy warm tone of her neck and shoulders begged for his touch, drawing him in between her thighs.

The seductive glow in her eyes cooled as he pulled the coat up over her shoulders. "I'm not cold." She shrugged the coat off.

"Tess, what are you really doing here?" He tried to step back from her, but she caught his hand, pulling it between her thighs. "I thought you hated me."

"I do, but I love fucking you." Her strong grip on his loosened tie brought his face down to hers. "I want you, Jack. No strings attached."

He didn't hear her last words, his blood whipping through his veins warp speed, pounding in his temples and throbbing in his crotch. No going back now, not with his fingers opening her labial lips and dipping deep inside her hot pussy. No way back with her fingers freeing his belt and zipper. He sucked in a breath as her fingers curled around his erection.

Her full moist lips pouted in a tease, making a small opening to let her tongue slide out, the damn thing flicking at him. She worked his hard dick to and fro, gasping with a laugh when he opened her with three fingers, her hips grinding into his fist.

He braced his weight with one hand, pushing forward to crush her lips in a deep, hungry kiss, forcing her mouth open to accept his tongue. She moaned, biting him playfully, toppling back on the hard oak to open her legs. He gazed at the woman offering her all to him.

"Damn you, Tessa." He pulled her legs apart and up to his waist, expecting to self-implode while she guided his cock to the glistening entrance of her pussy. From that point on, he lost all reason and desire to be noble. Hell with that. She took all of him, arching her hips and locking her arms around his neck, making those little noises she made just before reaching climax.

Distant sounds of things falling to the floor seemed natural while they worked hard to satisfy each other. She sucked his nipples and scratched his back, a fury to find release came through her nails and teeth. He thrust deep, hard and fast, deprivation and desire for her slapping away all niceties. The pressure of climax forced him to move against her forcefully, burying himself in her. Her back arched and she bucked against him, screaming against his neck, slowly dropping onto the desk. In a final powerful drive, he climaxed, fighting for breath and strength in his legs.

Several minutes passed before he spoke to her. "What now, baby?" He pulled her up to hug her close.

"I'll tell you after I use the powder room." She kissed him with a teasing smile. "Don't look so worried, Jack."

She got off the desk and headed for the washroom, glancing back over her shoulder when he found his voice. "I'm not worried, Tess. Just curious."

Who are you trying to kid, Savage? You hate the fact she leaves you and probably goes to someone else. What would be wrong with having her on those terms?

Everything.

He'd had his share of forgettable women, lied to more than one, but not this time. Something about Tessa filled his senses to the full and without her, he ran on empty.

He should tell her what he felt, not talk to her like a greasy barfly would. Hell no, she'd laugh in his face. Tessa didn't want him for anything other than a quick toss on his desk. Best to keep his mouth shut. Doing that got harder every day.

* * * *

Tessa sat on the chair that Jack's secretary had probably placed in the bathroom. She hated herself for practically raping him. She didn't want him that way.

Liar. You want him any way it takes.

Then why was she so miserable? She knew the answer and it hurt. She wanted him to come to her with all that force and heat. She loved him, wanted him to feel the same about her. She rose, suddenly feeling cheap and dirty. No wonder he screwed her when she tricked him with her naked body.

A light rap on the door interrupted her dark thoughts.

"I'll be right out." She hesitated, then added brightly, "Hand me my coat, Jack. My lipstick's in the pocket."

He stood in the doorway and held the coat out, waiting for her to slide her arms in the sleeves. "You've been in here quite awhile. Everything okay?"

"Of course." Her voice wavered. "You know how women are."

"Do you want me to drive you somewhere, babe? Home maybe to get some clothes?"

"I have clothes in my car." This escapade hadn't ended as she'd dreamed. "Where I'm going, no clothes are required."

"Are you trying to worry me?"

"You asked, Mister."

Why did he have to look at her so intently, his dark eyes delving into her soul as no one else ever had? Could he see she had humiliated herself, and he did nothing to make her feel whole again?

He walked away, leaning over to pick up the pens, files, and his briefcase they had scattered in the heat of passion. "I asked because I care about what happens to you."

"Don't worry, Jack." Desire to slump on the floor gripped her, but she crossed the floor on steady legs. "I'm going home. Sorry to have made a nuisance of myself." She blew him a kiss. "Happy birthday."

He did the thing she'd hoped for, came to her and caught her hand, his smile warm. "Thank you for thinking of me, Tess."

Damn fool. He was all she thought of.

Chapter Twelve

After making the mistake of a lifetime, Tessa vowed never to run after Jack again. She accepted the painfully clear fact that he wasn't ready for her now. Perhaps he never would be. His easy acceptance of her leaving his office the last time had nearly broke her heart.

Four in the morning and she still hadn't closed her eyes, trying to remember every word he'd said. Why do that? He'd made no comment other than suggest she put some clothes on. She groaned, remembering the great sex. It had never been anything but a desire to be close to someone, even for just a little while. But with Jack, she knew she was in his strong arms and sharing the sensuality that only comes with love.

Get over it. You'll find someone else. Forget that. They won't be Jack. It had been weeks and he hadn't made any effort to heat things back up. She was taking her degree and moving on. To where? She'd know when she got there.

Getting her brain into the books had taken some effort, but Tessa had wanted to finish one thing in her life. If not, her newfound self-esteem would flatten like a popped balloon.

She glanced around the gleaming clean kitchen and remembered the chocolate éclairs in the refrigerator. When she opened the door, it occurred to her that she had eaten nothing but junk food for days. She was hungry for real food.

Standing in the open refrigerator door, licking the éclair's creamy filling, Tessa frowned. The pastry could never fill the hunger clawing at her every nerve.

Call him, fool. You are dying to hear his voice.

She grabbed the phone off the counter and tabbed in his home number. It rang three times before he picked up. His hello kissed her ear and the tears started.

No, you can't do this anymore. Hang up, fool.

Cutting off the connection hurt as if she'd burned her hand. The ache in her heart screamed to get out. How could she survive without a reason to live?

She sat in the dark, for the first time unafraid of the shadows and night noises.

The phone rang, but she ignored it. Drake was probably checking to see if she'd turned in all her homework. He'd told her how proud he was of her and they had to have a celebratory dinner soon. She sighed with resignation. Her brother had been right all the time, and she'd fought him every step of the way.

She rose and went to the bedroom, stripping off her clothes to flop nude on the bed.

After tossing and turning for several hours, she gave up and went into the bathroom to shower. Today, she wouldn't be late.

While she dried her body, the memory of the Blue Bird Café drifted into her thoughts. What would it harm if she drove there for an early breakfast?

She felt deep scorn for herself. If he was there, what would she say and do? God, why couldn't she deal with life like an adult?

* * * *

Jack sat on the edge of his bed, his emotions going in crazy directions. Why hadn't she said anything when he answered the phone? Why hadn't he called her back?

The answer was too complicated for a mere mortal like him. Damn, the woman kept him torn up, her idea of a joke tearing his balls out. How long had it been since he'd relaxed, had a date? He couldn't remember.

He lay back down on the bed and stared at the ceiling. *Okay, figure this out or commit yourself to a mental hospital.*

He rationalized every aspect of the fireball relationship he'd had with Tessa. Constant upheaval, cops, car accidents, funerals for assholes, and sex. What else could a guy ask for?

He groaned and pulled a pillow over his head to cover the mournful sound.

What do you have without her? Order, routine, dull evenings alone, and the never-ending yearning to hear her voice. He missed Tessa and all the uproar she brought with her.

Lights from a passing car lit up his bedroom. Five in the morning and he hadn't gotten back to sleep after her call.

This is fucking madness.

He hugged his pillow and closed his eyes before allowing the truth to burst in his mind. He loved Tessa and it mattered little what she brought to the table, as long as she loved him. He had to find out.

With hard resolution, he got up and turned on the bathroom light, but not before he stepped on something. Under his foot was a gold cylinder, winking in the light.

This had to be a good sign. Tessa's lipstick.

Good sign or not, he had to find her and damn quick. His life had become laughable and he needed her with him. He gave thought to the fact that she may not feel the same as he did. Come to think of it, she'd never said how she felt about him.

Yanking some jeans and a shirt from the closet, he grimaced. Didn't make a damn bit of difference. He would say it to her pretty face and wait for the explosion. Didn't all men go through this?

He pulled his clothes on and looked at the clock. Hell, way too early to spring this kind of load on the princess.

Like hell it is.

He locked the door and sprinted to the garage. So this was what love did to a man. He hadn't felt so good in his whole life.

Get ready baby, your life is about to change.

Chapter Thirteen

Still in her bathrobe, Tessa stood at the top of the stairs, trying to see who stood at her front door through the slot windows. Identifying the person was impossible. Maybe they would go away.

Insistent knocking on the door followed several more rounds of the bell.

"Tessa."

Relief flooded through her when she recognized the voice. Hurrying down the stairs, she opened the door to see Jack on her doorstep.

What should she do, or say? Calm down.

"Jack." She pulled her robe together and stepped back to let him in. "Is something wrong?"

He stayed where he was for several seconds before answering. "We need to talk, Tessa."

This was different, not bossy or ringing with warning. Her nerves wound tight with apprehension. "Have you decided to go back to Arizona?"

He laughed and tugged on the belt of her robe. "Are you running me out of town?"

"Never." She inched closer to him, covering his hand with hers. "Even if you never want to be with me."

His arms eased around her. "I want one thing, Tessa. You." He tipped her chin up, his smile warm and sweet. "I love you. I want to be with you for the rest of my life. I'll do everything in my power to make this work. The question is, what exactly are your intentions toward me?"

She stammered, having always thought the words would flow smooth and sexy. "I feel so passionately about you I can't describe what's in my heart." This was real, he truly had said the words she'd longed to hear, and now she trembled with emotion. "I love you. I just want to make you happy." She held his face in her hands, gazing into his eyes. "Don't ever change your mind, Jack. I won't let you go."

He squeezed her tight, groaning with obvious pleasure to see his prospective bride's robe fall to the floor. "Don't change a thing for me, Tessa."

THE END

www.bettywomack.net

ABOUT THE AUTHOR

I have always loved books. Reading was a passion early in my life. I read everything the famous and not so famous authors wrote. I was a die hard historical romance-only fan until I found contemporary to be just as satisfying to read. I began the rocky journey to publication, blind to all the rules and terribly afraid of rejection. With the help of patient critique partners and surviving more than a few disappointments, my first full-length novel was accepted for publication.

I live in the Midwest, and enjoy being near my two adult children and my wonderful wildflower garden. I will never stop being delighted by the notes sent by a reader commenting on my work. Hearing from readers is important to me. I want to write stories that stay with you for a long while. I do it all for you.

Also by Betty Womack

Siren Classic: *Palace of the Jaguar*
Siren Classic: *The Stetson*
Siren Classic: *Her Private John*
Siren Classic: *Hot for Nick*
Siren Classic: *Uncut*
PolyAmour: *Hot Wired*
BookStrand Mainstream: *Hot Zone*

Available at
BOOKSTRAND.COM

Siren Publishing, Inc.
www.SirenPublishing.com